CAT
on a
WIRE

ALSO BY SHAW COLLINS

CASSIA LEMON MYSTERIES

Cat on a Wire

Cat Dancer

Cat and Mouse

———

www.ShawCollins.com

SHAW COLLINS

CAT on a WIRE

A Cassia Lemon Mystery

GREENLEES PUBLISHING

Published by Greenlees Publishing, contact@greenleespublishing.com

eBook ISBN-13: 978-1-951098-15-5

Paperback ISBN-13: 978-1-951098-16-2

Large Print Paperback ISBN-13: 978-1-951098-17-9

Artwork by Kudryashka, Deposit Photos

For Family,
as always

CHAPTER 1

Cassia Lemon tripped over a box laying on the living room floor and stubbed her toe. She grabbed it while howling like a banshee and hopped around, trying to not fall into another box, which was difficult since the entire floor was covered with boxes in various states of packing. How could she, a poor college student, own so much crap? It was ridiculous.

At least it hid the ugly brown carpet and ancient plywood cabinets of the University Palisade Rolling Thunder apartments. The name sounded like something a teenager who watched too many bad movies came up with, and the complex was run with the same efficiency. The owner had a captive audience with the students of the nearby university and knew it. Cassia often thought the bars on the doors and windows were just too spot-on meta for the situation. But it did have a few benefits, like Cassia now knew what the cuisine of at least ten different countries smelled like. Most of the time it was a good thing.

Cassia managed to hop over to the one end of the couch that wasn't covered in cardboard and clothes and packing paper. Flopping back onto the old paisley cushions, she pulled her foot into herself and continued the wailing. It didn't hurt that much, but there was something so satisfying about voicing her frustration. It had been a frustrating day.

Moving was never easy. It was especially not easy when you had no money for movers, or car, or pizza. Was it even a move without pizza? Cassia was tired of hard. She wanted an easy button.

A big, fat, red, easy button.

One that delivered pizza, and rides, and sexy strong movers. Or any movers. She'd even take little old lady movers, cripes she didn't care, as long as there was someone to help her. Actually, it might be kind of funny to watch little old ladies tottering around with her boxes.

Was she a bad person? Probably. It'd still be funny.

Besides, even little old ladies like pizza.

While she was daydreaming, could they bring someone to deal with international moves and bureaucratic paperwork?

Moving to Puerto Rico wasn't exactly international, but it wasn't down the road either. Plus, it was dang expensive. She didn't have parents to drop her stuff off with, or take her to the airport, or even unbelievably to fly with her to college.

But she'd made it—at least through undergrad—on her own, and now she was off to grad school. A promised easy button for life. A big fancy degree that said she was something.

But so far, it was nothing but a big pain in the ass. And if she wanted to howl about it, she was going to dang well howl about it.

Bang! Bang!

Or maybe not.

Apparently, Ted, her next door neighbor, didn't like howling.

"What? That's all I get?" Cassia yelled to the wall behind her. "No running to see if I'm alright?"

"You're alright enough to yell," Ted's muffled voice came

from the wall. It wasn't that muffled, though. Calling these university apartments cheap would be like calling Mount Kilimanjaro a hill.

"Yeah, so?" Cassia said.

"I can't concentrate on my game," Ted said.

"You could come help me pack," Cassia said.

"You going to take me to paradise?" Ted asked. Cassia could just see him on his couch hunched over his coffee table, still in his brown delivery uniform and his now suddenly cool-again mullet, firing away madly at the game controller. He was either twenty or forty, somehow it was impossible to tell.

"You know I can't do that," Cassia said.

"Pack yourself then," Ted said.

"Some friend you are," Cassia said.

Ted didn't reply. Cassia refused to think it was because he wasn't her friend.

Cassia put her foot back down and looked at the pile of stuff on her couch next to her. An old bathrobe sat half-in and half-out of a box, along with some sweaters and clothes she didn't remember getting at the thrift shop off-campus. This was a box for donations. All her cold weather clothing that hopefully she would never, ever, need again.

She grabbed the box and pulled it close, shoving the sweaters down and trying to fit everything else on the couch inside of it so she could tape it shut. It was just a bit too much contents, and the top flaps refused to meet in the middle so she could tape them.

Cassia stubbornly crawled on top of the box, teetering dangerously on top of the couch, and bounced down on the stubbornly resistant sweaters and terrycloth. The box springs of the old couch squeaked in protest.

"I hate to interrupt your good time there, but your fancy boss is here," Ted said, the drollness in his voice clear even through the wall.

"It's not a good time," Cassia snapped.

"I'm not judging, though your boss might."

Boss? The words sank in. What boss? Her advisor? Jonass Birum? He'd only been here once, and that was a special occasion for her graduation and her full-ride acceptance into the program where she would get her prized PhD. Pretty Hot Deal, as she liked to call it.

Cassia looked up mid-bounce, tape gun held high, as her advisor's face appeared on the other side of her barred screen door. He looked concerned and distracted. His light brown and patched cardigan made him look like a discount Mr. Rogers. His wildly unkempt brown hair flying in every direction didn't help. As always, she had the urge to comb it down flat. He held a large box filled with pictures and papers and even a tiny toy telescope sticking out of it.

She had a telescope just like that.

She looked again. Wait, that *was* her telescope. What was he doing with her box of stuff?

Juggling the box to one arm, he knocked on the side of the screen and gave her a watery smile. Before she could leap off the couch, he grabbed the door handle and tried to open it. It was locked, of course. Middle of the day or not, this was a place to keep the doors locked.

"Coming," Cassia said, throwing aside the tape gun and jumping off the couch. She picked her way across the living room. Hopefully he would back up so she could come outside. There was just too much stuff in here.

But of course he didn't. As soon as she flipped the deadbolt on the screen, he pulled open the door and stepped inside, the box he held nearly pushing Cassia backwards over the box of pots behind her.

"Wait a minute, wait a minute," Cassia said, quickly backing up by stepping and sliding over things behind her. "What are you doing here?"

"Well… well, I was on my way home anyhow and thought I'd save you the trip getting this," Professor Birum said, or Professor Beer as she often thought.

Cassia narrowed her eyes at him. He lived in the fancier places by the river. Exactly the opposite direction of the sprawling student apartments on the far side of campus.

He shifted his weight from foot to foot under her gaze, then shoved the box at her after finding no place to put it down around him.

"Thanks," Cassia said, taking the box from him. "Just what I need, another box of stuff."

"Well, it does have your research. I thought you'd want that."

"It does, it does. I was just dreading trying to take it home on the bus." He really had done her a favor, Cassia grudgingly admitted to herself.

Cassia looked helplessly to her disastrously half packed kitchen, then back at Professor Birum. They stared at each other.

"Thanks again," Cassia said. "I'd offer you something, but… we could walk to the corner store for coffee?"

"No, thanks… I should get home, Ellie's expecting me," Professor Birum said, turning to grab the door and then turning back to Cassia indecisively. He looked guiltier than a cat caught with a mouse in his mouth.

"What?" Cassia finally demanded, after watching the man dance back and forth for another few seconds, more frustration in her voice than she meant to show.

He flapped his arms helplessly. "I just wanted to make sure you're all right. I feel really bad. It's shocking even. I already asked the dean, and there's no money this year, but maybe next year. Really. Who would've thought? I mean, it's been there for so long. Anything the military makes you'd expect to last for a long time, but apparently didn't last… for a long time. Or not long enough. I lost ten days on my own schedule over it. It's crazy."

Cassia's mouth hung open. That was more words from Professor Birum in one string than she heard in practically every lecture he'd ever done. Or ever. The man was losing it.

Then just as quickly, the river of words from him stopped. He stared at her.

She waited for more, but he just stood there with his arms drooping by his side.

"You expected what to last so long?" Cassia finally prompted.

"The telescope," Professor Birum said.

Cassia's eyes slid down to her toy telescope. It looked fine. Whatever telescope could he be talking about? The university's telescope was an old thing on the edge of the city, making it useless except for a tourist attraction. What could have shaken the man so?

"Yes," Professor Birum said, catching her looking down at her box.

Cassia looked back up at him confused. "The toy?"

He shook his head and reached down to grab the cellophane and styrofoam framed poster nestled in the box next to the toy telescope. It was the poster she'd bought on internship two years ago. Holding it gingerly, he turned it around for her to stare at the Arecibo telescope, the world's largest single dish radio telescope, nestled in the rolling hills of Puerto Rico, its gigantic Gregorian receiver hanging low like the world's largest dingleberry over the thousand-foot dish.

"What?" Cassia whispered, dread suddenly filling her tummy.

"It broke," Professor Birum said hoarsely.

"Yeah, that doesn't look fixable," Ted said as he handed her a beer. Cassia took it without looking, barely hearing his words. She sat gap mouthed on his micro-suede couch, staring at his huge TV currently showing the picture of the Arecibo telescope from the news release. Instead of a beautiful, if somewhat dirty white dish with a massive receiver above it, it looked like a bowl of noodles from the local Pho shop. Twisted metal girders piled high in the middle of the dish, topped with gigantic metal ropes that had all snapped and coiled around the grounds like terrifying snakes.

The cable supports had snapped. Or one had, and the rest had said forget this work and soon followed, sending the entire beautiful, expensive array of equipment suspended over the dish crashing down onto it. Through it, actually.

The dish wasn't usable. The receiver was total trash.

And so were her graduate plans.

Her work on low latitude galactic clouds had won her a spot there in Arecibo. A *resident* spot. A rare, hard-to-find spot, especially for a graduate student. And all the other schools in the nation had made their choice of students for the year. They were full up, or at least out of money. There was nowhere else for her to go. Her funding was tied to that telescope.

That very dead telescope.

Ted sat next to her. He nudged her with one hairy knee, exposed by the cheesy shorts of his uniform, and tried to click bottles with her. She didn't respond, her bottle held limply in her hand.

Eying her slack face, Ted gently removed the bottle from her hand and put it on the coffee table. "Nevermind then," he sighed when she didn't respond.

"I already put in my notice on the apartment. They've rented it already," Cassia said in a monotone.

"Think of it as a chance to travel. A vacation," Ted said,

sinking into the couch next to her, and then awkwardly slapped her on the back.

She glared at him. "Vacations cost money. Especially year-long ones."

"Not that much," he said unconvincingly.

"Eating does," she said.

"Picky, picky. Here," he said, pulling an envelope from the inner pocket of his jacket, "this came for you and I signed for it while in the office. Guy wanted to close up early and I know how you are about getting your mail."

She had sort of terrorized the office staff while waiting for the letter about her funding request. They just didn't take the mail seriously in that stupid California-sunshine-and-always-happy apartment office. Some things were serious.

Cassia pulled her eyes from the screen and looked at the proffered envelope in Ted's hand. It was on thick textured cream paper. It was also really dirty.

"How long have you had that?" she asked.

Looking away, Ted coughed. "Not long."

She ripped open the envelope, struggling because of the well-taped post office confirmation paperwork attached to it. Pulling out a single sheet of matching cream paper, she scanned it quickly. Then again. "No way," she said under her breath.

She let the paper droop while she stared at the TV again. Then she read the letter a second time, going slow this time.

"What?" Ted asked, trying to peer over her shoulder to read the letter. She leaned away from him.

"Come on, don't be like that," he said petulantly.

She glanced at him. "Right, sorry, sorry… habit." She gave him the paper to read himself.

He, too, read it twice. "Wait, this says you just inherited…"

"That's right," she leapt up, feeling some energy for the first time that day. "I just inherited a mansion! I'm rich!"

He stared at her, then stood himself, mirroring her energy. "Well then, problem solved!" He grabbed his beer bottle off the coffee table and held it out to her. Cassia grabbed her own beer from the table and clinked its neck to the neck of his bottle.

"Problem solved!" She tipped the bottle back and drank.

CHAPTER 2

"Problem solved, my ass," Cassia muttered under her breath as she drove the cranky old twelve-foot all-in-one rental truck down the windy interstate. She sat on the cracked vinyl of the seat, high above the pavement, bouncing along on the shot springs, feeling very much like a child in a high chair.

It didn't help that the interior of the cab looked like it came right out of the fifties, complete with push button controls. She wouldn't have been surprised if she had pulled off the facing of the control panel to find glass tubes. This truck was a museum piece, not a roadworthy vessel for her great journey. Those rental people were crooks. They probably pulled this unit from the junkyard.

Whatever.

As long as it got her to Creepy Valley or whatever-it-was Minnesota. Forgotten Valley. Farmer Valley. Oh, whatever. She'd programmed it into her phone that hung from the heat exhaust grill in the middle of the dash by twist ties because she'd forgotten to order a phone mount in time. Not that she had a lot of money for that. And she didn't have to worry about the heat affecting her phone, because the heat didn't work either.

She'd discovered that this morning in twenty degree weather outside her motel in the middle of Nebraska. At least the truck had started, even if it did wheeze and sputter for a few minutes first.

Cassia growled to herself, hunching down further into the seat to get her neck more fully into her jacket. First stop at this new place was going to be for winter clothes. Real winter clothes.

It was flipping September. This was ridiculous.

If her long-lost aunt Mildred wasn't dead already, she'd kill her.

Who gives someone a mansion as a gift and then puts ridiculous conditions on it like must live there for a year and get to know locals and the rest of the stuff in that crazy will?

And where was this generous aunt when Cassia was struggling with bills and learning how to live after her parents died? This whole thing was weird.

But there was still a carrot in the whole mess. If Cassia fulfilled all the conditions of the will, she'd have a huge house free and clear. Even for a house in the middle of nowhere, that had to be worth something. She could sell it just in time to get on with her life in astrophysics. Next year she'd get a spot in the prestigious Cornell program where Carl Sagan had taught if it killed her. Cornell had access to telescope time all over the world. Never again would she make the mistake of tying her fortunes to one place. She may be young, but she learned fast.

Ted had thought it was great how well it worked out with the house and stuff. He'd said he'd help her drive out and all, but he had his work. Somehow his work had never come up when he'd asked about her taking him to a tropical island. Figures.

Cassia didn't think all that great after reading the list of conditions in the will. Frankly, Mildred sounded like a control freak. If she had had the power, Cassia thought Mildred would have brought down the Arecibo telescope single-handedly just to get her niece to do what she wanted her to do. Cassia shuddered. Her thoughts were really getting away from her. Some little old lady in Podunk Minnesota had no power to bring down an internationally famous telescope. Right?

She straightened in the seat, stretching her back the best she could without letting go of the ridiculously large steering wheel. If the truck had power steering, it was the wimpiest power steering she'd ever dealt with. She didn't dare let the wheel get too far off or she'd not be able to muscle it back to straight before ending up in the ditch, or worse, in incoming traffic.

The flat prairie lands slowly gave way to a few trees here and there in neat lines between fields, then into patches of woods. A few hours later, after the first woods appeared, pine trees took over, filling the landscape. The air grew noticeably cooler. Snow even dusted the ground in patches. Cassia huffed.

Finally, a tall wooden sign next to the highway with a huge painted lumberjack with a red plaid shirt let her know she'd reached Forgotten Valley, Minnesota. He grinned an idiotic smile. Perhaps it was three full days of driving that ancient beast, or her aching back, but that grin made Cassia want to stop the truck and kick the painted sign in the ankles.

It definitely was the long days of driving making her crabby, because that didn't sound rational at all, even in her own head.

The town itself was small, consisting of only a few long blocks along a main road. Old-fashioned stores with huge windowpanes lined both sides of the block, every single window filled with carefully crafted scenes. The plumbing shop had a full-blown diorama featuring a toilet and shiny brass bathroom fixtures, the kitchen shop had beautifully matched pots and decorations over a lacquered enameled stove that looked to be a hundred years old. There was even a five-and-dime with mannequins that looked right out of the fifties.

Cassia patted the dash panel of her truck as she drove it slowly down the main drag. "Well, Truckster, it looks like you'll fit right in here." Yeah, Truckster wasn't the most creative name, but she'd not felt too generous to the vehicle when she'd first laid eyes on it. Maybe she'd come up with a better name. It had carried her two thousand miles without dying on her.

The plan was to have a late lunch before trying to find the mansion. The final will instruction packet she'd gotten had directions from Main Street and a note telling her to be sure to not lose the directions. As it turned out, the house itself was not in any mapping software she'd tried to use, a feat she found rather impressive.

Getting anywhere with written directions required more mental energy than she could muster on an empty stomach.

Lucking out with a spot large enough to park the twelve-foot monstrosity, Cassia parked the beast and hopped out. It felt eerily quiet once the chugging engine shut off. She adjusted her hat and pulled on some gloves. The air didn't feel as cold as in Nebraska, but it was nothing like the warmth of the California she'd just left. A few people walked on the sidewalks down the block, but no one looked at her. Good sign.

Turned out, there was only one restaurant in town. Smith's Deli and Diner.

Cassia pulled open the door of the diner, nestled between the five-and-dime and a woman's clothing shop, and was greeted by the ringing of a string of bells attached to the top of the door.

Booths lined the fronts of both windows. A light blue, gold-speckled Formica countertop curved around an island in the center of the space, complete with an enclosed plastic pie display on one end. Round stools lined the counter. The whole place looked exactly like what Cassia imaged it did when it was constructed in the 1950s. Or earlier. Apparently, remodeling was not a thing around here.

"Greetings!" a cheerful voice called out. "Take a seat anywhere. The booths are nice, but cold right now."

The voice belonged to a cheerful woman about Cassia's age wearing a light blue waitress uniform complete with a blue skirt covered by a frilly white apron, along with black combat boots and thick wool black stockings. Her hair, dark, was styled asymmetrically in the hottest fashion right out of social media. Or a Japanese manga.

Confused by the woman's appearance, Cassia touched her own hair, then looked around and picked the booth in the middle of the row in front of the windows. The rest of the window booths were empty. She slid into the seat, sliding easily over the vinyl. She could see everyone in the diner from her vantage point. Unfortunately, that meant everyone could see her as well. She grabbed a menu from the stand by the napkin dispenser and laid it flat out on the table, willing herself not to stare at the assorted people inside the diner. Her earlier glance had revealed people of all ages, from toddlers to old men hunched over the counter. Did no one have to work in this town?

Cassia's face burned. Apparently, not everyone had the same decision not to stare.

The woman came over, pad and pen in hand. "Hi there. I'm Genevieve. What can I get ya?"

"What's good?" Cassia asked, stalling for time. The menu was surprisingly huge.

Genevieve tapped her pen on her bottom lip. She glanced back at the kitchen, then leaned in to Cassia. "Honestly, chef's choice will get you the best service. And the freshest ingredients. He takes it as sort of a dare."

Cassia frowned.

"You don't have any food allergies, do ya?"

Cassia slowly shook her head.

"Great," Genevieve said, standing up straight again. "Trust me, you'll be happy." She whirled and started walking back to the counter.

"Wait," Cassia called after her.

"A drink, right?" Genevieve said over her shoulder.

"Yeah—"

"Gotcha covered, also—"

"Chef's choice," Cassia muttered in unison with Genevieve as she slouched down into the seat. This wasn't the most promising start. Chef's choice was something she imagined only the highest choice restaurants in Manhattan would have, at least that's what she thought from watching the ancient movies Ted favored.

A moment later, a steaming mug of golden liquid with a cinnamon stick poking out slid in front of Cassia. It smelled amazing—like Christmas morning and cookies. Cassia reached out for it and then glanced up at Genevieve's amused expression.

"I thought you might like it," Genevieve said.

Gingerly, Cassia blew on the hot liquid and took a sip. It was the most delicious thing she'd ever tasted. The spicy flavor rolled around her mouth. If it hadn't been so warm, she'd have drunk the whole thing in one shot.

"Do I ever," Cassia said. "What is it?"

"That, I can't tell you," Genevieve said, "except it has a ton of spices and cooks on the back stove all day long. I swear that's why half the people are here. There's a two mug limit."

A limit on food?

Cassia raised her eyebrows.

Genevieve stared at Cassia's green wool captain's hat with its cheesy bill and fake braid. "Like your hat," Genevieve said.

Cassia pulled the hat off and shoved it down next to her on

the seat. It had been a dollar at the thrift shop. It was warm, but now she wished she'd held off for something a little less seventies grandpa. "Thanks. I like your… uniform."

"Thanks. Me too. I wear it ironically," Genevieve said, giving Cassia a brilliant smile.

What does that even mean, to wear something ironically? They were the same age, but suddenly Cassia had the same feeling she'd always had in grade school, that the other kids were speaking a language she didn't understand. "Oh, I'm sure you're doing it quite well then."

Cassia looked away, gazing out the window, hoping Genevieve took the hint. Instead, Genevieve shifted her weight on one hip and tapped the table with her pen.

"So dish, why are ya here?" Genevieve asked.

"To eat," Cassia said, reluctantly bringing her gaze back to Genevieve.

Genevieve waved that away. "Yeah, yeah, yeah. No one comes to this town just to eat. Why are you here?" She spoke the last words slowly, as if Cassia was hard of hearing or something.

What the heck. They'd all find out soon enough anyway.

"I inherited a place just outside of town. The Mandress mansion, or something. Of course with my luck it's actually a run-down shack with a sign saying mansion tacked on the front…" Cassia's words ground to a halt as she noticed the staring eyes of everyone in the diner. All of them. Every single person was staring at her now. Even the kid in the high chair.

Dead silence filled the diner.

Cassia looked back up at Genevieve. "That's why," she said in a small voice.

Genevieve cleared her throat, the smile of a moment ago replaced with a pained look. "Well, that's interesting. Your food will be ready in a minute, I'm sure." And like that she was gone, leaving Cassia to stare after her gap mouthed. The others in the diner quickly looked away and started talking amongst themselves, filling the silence with the dull roar of chatter.

Cassia's meal came, a scrumptious feast of perfectly grilled tenderloin over a bed of wilted greens and a side of chopped fruit of pinks and whites and yellows in a sour sauce. Cassia had a hard time enjoying it though, constantly aware of the glances and whispers in her direction. She hunched over her meal and ate it quickly.

Genevieve left her check without a word.

Cassia paid at the counter and left. As the door shut behind her and the tinkling of the door bells cut off, she looked into the diner's window as she walked past. Those inside had dropped all pretense of not staring at her. They looked like a shocked Greek chorus.

CHAPTER 3

Cassia bounced in her seat as the truck went over pothole after pothole. She gripped the wheel and ground her teeth as she thought of every single one of her dishes in the back probably broken and rattling in their boxes. She turned her phone's volume up, blasting *Not Today* by her favorite band to cover the noise of any of her belongings smashing to their bitter ends in the boxes in the back of the truck. She'd put on her battle music track list after getting out of the diner.

This inheritance was already turning out to be terrible and she'd not even been to the place yet. What was wrong with those people back there?

The directions to the house lay open on her lap and she glanced down at them from time to time. Her slow speed helped her not run off the road, if what was there could be called a road. A long beige gravel path twisted between trees, challenging the turning radius of the truck. Branches smashed into the high box of the vehicle. Clearly, nothing large had passed through here recently. Had anything at all passed through here recently?

Perhaps Aunt Mildred rode a broomstick through the trees on her way into town.

Cassia shook her head. Her mind was really getting away from her.

Finally, the trees thinned, and the road took one last turn into an open field that led up to a huge black and gray structure. The building appeared to be large enough to cover a quarter of a city block and was three stories high.

Cassia took her foot off the gas and let the truck come to a halt. It idled roughly and the exhaust popped its unhappiness at being stopped. Annoyed at the noise, Cassia flicked off the ignition. She wanted a moment just to stare at this place. This could not possibly be hers. It looked like something out of a Gothic novel, perched on the edge of some dark moors, and not nestled in the middle of America.

Opening the truck door, Cassia jumped down and walked toward the building. Low gray clouds hung like gigantic bubbles over it and the entire clearing. Dark shadows filled the surrounding trees.

Cassia crossed her arms and glared at the surroundings. "Okay, universe, this is just ridiculous. I am not in the mood for this. Show me something nice." Because, really, this was just too much. She did not live in the eighteen hundreds, and she certainly was not looking to meet someone named Heathcliff.

Stubbornly, Cassia held her position, then tapped her foot for extra emphasis.

"Universe!" Cassia yelled suddenly. The yell echoed through the clearing in the trees, sending birds in flight. The breeze picked up, dragging the clouds above, which then parted to let a ray of sun shoot down and hit the house.

Cassia jumped back, dropping her arms from her cocky position. "Well, I didn't really expect an answer." Putting her hands up as if to stop whatever was happening, she twirled around as if looking for someone responsible for the wind and the sun. There was no one. "I don't think I'm going to do that again," she muttered to herself.

She pulled her jacket down and straightened her shoulders, then walked to the house.

What had at first appeared to be gray and black was just an old dark blue paint job trimmed with really dirty white. Poorly made siding patches lay nailed over sections of the house that she assumed were damaged. Everywhere overgrown bushes and trees crowded against the building. The house wasn't quite as ominous as it had seemed at first. Just not well cared for.

Cassia walked the perimeter of the house, avoiding the occasional piles of black walnut shells that must've been left by some busy squirrel. The first side of the house looked much the same as the front, three stories tall, with ornate molding around the tall and skinny windows. She turned the corner around to see the back of the house and gasped. Not at all looking like the rest of the house, a section only two stories tall jetted out toward the back woods with a large sectioned black metal dome covering it.

"No, way," Cassia said. "No, way."

What on earth would something like that be doing in a house like this?

She ran toward the dome section, looking for an entryway. There was one door with a large brass handle. She grabbed it and twisted. Locked. She shook the door anyway. It didn't give. It didn't even budge.

Neither did the small door on the back of the house that looked like it probably came off a rear kitchen.

Running around to the front of the house, she bounded up the stairs and reached for the handle, only to skid to a stop as the door opened before she could grasp it. She thought her heart was going to explode in her chest. "What the heck?"

A tiny woman dressed in an old-fashioned teal suit with a pillbox hat perched jauntily on her tightly pulled back red hair stood in the doorway and beamed at her. Her cheeks were round and rosy. She looked cheerful and welcoming despite the severe bun of her hairstyle. Again, the strange combination of young woman and really old-fashioned clothes. Was there some dress code Cassia wasn't aware of?

Cassia blinked at her. "Who are you?"

"I'm Sarah Rheton," the woman answered then went back to smiling.

"Okay. But who are you?" Cassia asked again.

The woman cocked her head at Cassia, not understanding. "I'm Sarah—"

Cassia held up a hand. "Yes, Sarah, but why are you here?"

"I'm the housekeeper. You must be Miss Lemon, if I'm not mistaken," Sarah said.

Cassia nodded slowly. She threw one hand up and put it on her hip while looking around awkwardly. "Um… ahh, no one said anything about a housekeeper."

"I come with the house," Sarah said, still not losing her smile. Cassia was beginning to hate that smile.

"I don't have any money to pay a housekeeper," Cassia said.

"It's all been taken care of. It's part of your year trial. Miss Mandress took care of it," Sarah said.

Oh, good old aunt Mildred. Of course she did. Would it have been too much to put this in the will as well? Of course it would.

"Great, wonderful. Nice to meet you," Cassia said. How did one talk to a housekeeper? What exactly was a house-keeper? "It's a beautiful house," Cassia said, feeling ridiculous with her praise. It didn't look beautiful at the moment, but what did one say? *This place is a dump and are you responsible?* She made herself look around while trying to check out Sarah Rheton from the corner of her eye. Did the woman lived there? She looked about thirty, but had the polish and confidence of a much older woman.

"Excuse me. I apologize for my bad manners. Please come in. We've been expecting you," Sarah said as she backed out of the doorway and motioned for Cassia to enter.

"We?" Cassia asked as she stepped inside the house.

The interior looked nothing like the outside. For one thing, it was spotless. Light blonde wood flooring filled the entryway and ran into the adjacent rooms on either side and up the double curves of the wide stairways in the entry. Light green and pastel blue paint covered the walls, trimmed with delicate white molding. Lemon and cream colored French style furniture with wooden legs and carved backs filled the rooms. It was as beautiful and pleasant on the inside as it was dark and ominous on the outside.

"Yes, well, we being Miss Mansfield and I," Sarah said.

"Miss Mansfield?" Cassia said distractedly, as she stared at the beautiful interior.

A tiny meow from below caught Cassia's attention. A delicate black cat arched at her ankles, looking like it was standing on tiptoe.

"Miss Mansfield," Sarah said.

"You call a cat Miss Mansfield?" Cassia asked. "Seems a bit formal."

The cat in question stepped on Cassia's feet with all four of its own. Cassia looked down to the sleek black face and brilliant orange-gold eyes. It rubbed against her while it firmly ground its paws into her feet. Cassia tried to back up so the cat would get off her shoes but it stubbornly kept getting back on.

"I believe Miss Mansfield likes her name very much," Sarah said.

"Okay, *Miss Mansfield*," Cassia said, emphasizing the name, "nice to meet you."

The cat gave one final rub of her cheek on Cassia's shin and then delicately stepped off of Cassia's shoes.

"What about you? Do you prefer Miss Rheton?" Cassia asked the housekeeper as she lifted a foot and rubbed it.

Sarah gave a melodic laugh and waved off Cassia's question. "Oh no, nothing formal. Sarah will do just fine, but thank you for asking, Miss Lemon."

"Cassia is fine. Cat for short with my friends, and you, of course, not that you're not my friend..." Cassia slapped a hand over her mouth.

Sarah laughed again. "No worries, dear. I knew what you meant. I guess it's good we don't call Miss Mansfield *cat*, now isn't it?"

Cassia pursed her lips as she looked at the cat now primly licking its front paw.

———

The long tube of the massive machine swung gracefully inside the dome, its gears clicking as the motors moved it smoothly heavenward, while a few sections of the dome retracted and stacked.

The telescope, for that was what it was, was polished and pristine, even if it was ancient. Its long tube alone gave its ancient pedigree away, being nothing like the squat barrels and precisely machined optics of the more modern versions of stargazing machinery. Despite its imposing length, the mirror of this unit was too small a diameter to contribute much to modern research, but it was still a beautiful thing.

Plus, it wasn't hampered by being installed over the sea of light pollution that was Los Angeles, unlike her old university's only facility.

Cassia walked inside the dome, staring up at the telescope mounted on its pedestal and motor, and around the beautiful dome. This was what she'd seen from the outside, but even seeing it in person, she couldn't believe such a thing was a part of the house.

The whole place looked like a museum piece. Long wood tables stood pressed against the outer edges of the dome, neatly arrayed with green shaded library lights that she bet were outfitted with red bulbs. Neat bookcases packed with tomes lines the walls. One large square table held a star chart weighted down with large round weights. The base of the table held an array of drawers, probably hiding more charts.

Jonass would shit a brick if he saw this.

Not that she was in the mood to tell him about it. At all. No funding her ass. Cassia had spent more than one all-nighter analyzing his data so he could make his publication deadlines. She hoped no one in the undergrad crew could easily take her place. Forget it; she didn't have to hope. She knew the other undergrads. Half of them were only in it because astrophysics majors didn't have to take the hardest classes the physics students did. The other half were not as desperate for funding as she had been. Unless some amazing freshman came in this coming year, Professor Jonass Birum was on his own.

Sarah let go of the control she'd been pressing by the doorway. "Do you like?"

"Yes, I love…" Cassia said. "It's rather random though, all the way out here. Did my aunt study astronomy?"

Sarah laughed her musical laugh. "Oh no, though she was insistent this place be as clean as all the rest of the house. We even had special cleaners come out, at least for a while." A dark look crossed Sarah's face and then was gone as quickly as it had come. "It was her father's. I guess that would be, oh I don't know, your great uncle? I'm not very good at genealogy and stuff like that. Anyway, it was quite fashionable one time to have star parties. You weren't truly part of the in set unless you had your own telescope and a visiting professor to explain it to all your guests."

Cassia stared at Sarah, not even sure what to say. "That doesn't even sound real. How rich are these people?"

Sarah walked to Cassia and patted her arm gently. "You mean you, my dear? This is your house, now, or will be. And I'm sorry to tell you I don't think there's much cash left. I do know our cleaning crew got smaller every year." She gave Cassia a look. "And I am well aware of how the outside of the house looks."

That was one mystery solved. Too bad this tour was adding so many others.

"But this is in the middle of nowhere? Northern Minnesota. I mean, what you're describing sounds like something that would happen in New York." Or nowhere. Cassia's head hurt. This was not at all what she'd been expecting. Just because there was a telescope here didn't make her feel all that much better about this enormous weird house in the middle of nowhere. Okay, maybe a little bit better, but this was all just so… strange.

"Senior Mandress was a very private man. I've heard it was quite the honor back in the day when anyone was lucky enough to receive an invitation to the house for one of his rare parties."

All of a sudden, a wave of sadness washed over Cassia. This would have been exactly the time she would have called her parents to ask them what exactly was going on with their strange family, and to give them a hard time for not telling her anything about her crazy aunt Mildred and apparently even crazier father, but that was not an option. Not now. She walked away from Sarah and swung her arms, trying to distract her body.

As she was passing by the open top of the dome she looked out. Her head came just above the bottom of the opening, giving her a nice view of the woods surrounding the house and the rather messy backyard. A flash caught her eye. She stopped and went back to the opening and stared out. It was several flashes. White and red lights reflected on the thicket of narrow trees by the side yard. Something was going on in the front yard. "Sarah, were you expecting anyone else?" she asked.

Sarah came running to the edge of the dome, her heels clicking on the polished wood floor to join Cassia peering out of the dome.

CHAPTER 4

Cassia and Sarah ran out the front door and onto the front lawn. A huge white police cruiser peeked out from behind Cassia's van, trapped in the twisting road and the trees, a fancy circular emblem emblazoned on the doors and the lights on top spinning. At least they hadn't turned on the sirens.

The cruiser looked brand-new and spotless, unlike Cassia's dirty white van that sat exactly where she had left it in the middle of the narrow road. She hadn't even bothered to shut the door, she now realized. From this angle, it didn't look good. Rather like a crime scene where the door had been wrenched open and the inhabitant dragged away.

Oops.

Cassia turned to Sarah, "Were you expecting the cops?"

Sarah shook her head.

A shadowy figure moved inside the cruiser. Finally, the door opened with a firm click and swung wide. A tall man emerged, with the shoulders of a football player and a tight shirt to show them off. He even had one of those old-fashioned hats Cassia thought only Canadian Mounties wore. He had it at a rakish angle tilted forward and shading his eyes.

He walked around the door and shut it. Having spied them, he gave them a nod and walked toward them.

Holy heavens, his pants were even tighter than his shirt.

This was like watching a men's magazine version of a cop walking toward them. No, better yet a women's magazine. Or an underwear company's advertisement.

This was not how cops were supposed to look. Or sheriffs. Whatever.

Cassia's mouth felt dry. She tried to swallow, but it was impossible. Her water jug was in the van, but she was not moving from her spot, not for a million bucks.

"Sarah, ma'am," the sheriff said as he reached them, nodding in acknowledgment at them both as he spoke. "Do you know anything about this van?" His voice was low and smooth. Distracted, Cassia stared at his Adam's apple, trying to think how it could make his voice that low.

"Sheriff Andrews, this is Miss Lemon, the new owner of Mandress. I believe that is her van," Sarah said smoothly.

"Ma'am... Miss Lemon," Sheriff Andrews said. "Can I get you to move your van?"

Cassia drew her eyes up from his Adam's apple to his eyes. They were a deep blue. Dang it, life is not fair. How did this man have all the things?

"Ma'am?" Sheriff Andrews asked again after a long moment.

Cassia shook her head. "Um, sorry, it's been a long day. Cat. You can call me Cat." He could call her anything. "You want something?"

He spoke again slowly this time, as if she was slow. This was beginning to be a theme. "If this is your van, you need to move it."

Wait, what?

The entire road was probably on the land of this house.

"Isn't that a private road?" Cassia asked, confused.

"That doesn't matter. Roads can't be blocked or otherwise encumbered so as to prevent emergency services," Sheriff Andrews said. He sounded like he was reciting some memorized section of the law.

"But this is a private road, is it not?" Cassia asked again. Were they talking about the same thing?

Sheriff Andrews drew himself up and crossed his arms. "It doesn't matter. In this county, we have rules, and they are rules for a good reason. Please move your van."

A record scratch rang through Cassia's head, replacing the chorus of angels that had been sounding until now around that man's presence. Was he just dictating that she move her van on her own property?

Oh yes he was.

Cassia inhaled to give a hot retort when Sarah laid a hand on her arm and smoothly replied, "Of course she will, Sheriff Andrews. She's just arrived and is probably a little tired from the long drive. So sorry to have bothered you. We'll get it moved right away." Cassia tried to pull her arm away from Sarah, but Sarah hung on with a steel grip as she gently stepped between the sheriff and Cassia.

The sheriff grabbed the bill of his hat and gave a tip to Sarah, and then Cat. Cassia didn't miss the warning in his eyes. This man was all sorts of weird.

He walked back to his vehicle, giving them a good show of just how tight his pants were, then got in and backed up through the twisting drive at an impressive pace, twisting and turning through the trees that Cassia had so inelegantly bashed through on her way in.

Cassia pulled her arm away from Sarah. "What was that all about?"

"Oh, that was nothing. Some people are just set in their ways," Sarah said. She smoothed back her intense red hair and turned to the house.

"Yes, but he was set in his ways about how things were done on the land *under my house*," Cassia said, running after Sarah.

"Really, dear. It's not that big a deal," Sarah said.

Cassia stopped walking and chewed her lip as she watched the housekeeper return to the gigantic mansion, neatly managing her heels in the overgrown grass and weeds. A cold breeze blew and sent a chill down her neck. She pulled her jacket close and wished once again with all her heart she was back in California.

———

Cassia walked into the kitchen. Fancy off-white countertops covered white cabinets with plain silver pulls. The kitchen was modern and clean, looking simple in the most expensive way possible. It even had one of those gigantic vents over the stove she'd seen in fancy magazines in the checkout line at the discount grocery.

A sink large enough to take a bath in dominated the back wall, along with a huge double window that hung over it. The window faced out into the blackness of the night. Cassia knew it faced the woods. Goosebumps rose on her scalp. Anything could be out there. She checked the sides of the windows. Dang it, not even a wisp of a curtain to pull across this. That was going to have to be fixed pronto. She was a city girl, not an expert at living in the woods, especially not in a big creepy house, but even she knew letting just anyone look into the house was not a good thing.

The kitchen was probably bigger than her whole entire apartment back in California. It was also the only warm spot in the house. Sarah had given her a short tour of the main level before leaving but had forgotten to tell her how to adjust the thermostat. Cassia was too hungry and tired to want to keep searching for it. Food would help her warm up.

Opening one of the massive doors of the double fridge, Cassia found it stuffed full of food and bags of produce. The other fridge door yielded a case of water with a note taped to it. *Frozen dinners in the freezer drawer in case you do not like cooking —Sarah.*

"Bonus points for Sarah," Cassia said to herself.

"Meow?" a tiny voice called from the floor. Cassia jumped.

"Holy cow, cat, you can't sneak up on me like that," Cassia said, looking down at the gleaming black face of her new roommate, Miss Mansfield. Miss Mansfield meowed again while reaching a paw out to step on Cassia's foot.

"Miss Mansfield, Miss Mansfield, my beautiful Miss Mansfield," Cassia said while backing up. The cat gave a satisfied meow and sat down.

"I suppose you're hungry too?" Cassia asked. Miss Mansfield blinked back.

A quick search of the cupboard revealed a lot of fancy dishes and glassware, and then behind one pantry door, an amazing stash of canned cat food. Rows and rows of the stuff. It looked like enough food to feed that tiny cat for year. Or more.

"I guess we know what you eat," Cassia said, pulling out a can. She popped the lid and put it down on the ground in front of Miss Mansfield. The cat gave a startlingly loud meow but did not move.

"What?" Cassia asked. "It's food. I guess it's what you eat."

An even angrier meow was Miss Mansfield's response.

Searching the cupboards again, Cassia found a dish and a fork and dumped the contents of the can onto the dish and spread it out. She reached to put the dish on the floor again, keeping an eye on Miss Mansfield as she did. As she suspected, as the dish lowered to the floor, the cat opened its mouth to complain. Cassia swiftly raised the dish again. Okay, not the floor. Looking around, she spied a small section of counter that was probably meant to be a desk. "This will be your own personal dining table from now on." She put the dish of cat food on it. Miss Mansfield primly walked over to the counter, jumped up and started eating.

Cassia filled a bowl full of water and put it down for Miss Mansfield.

One task done. Now for herself.

Frozen meals packed the generously sized freezer section. Cassia clapped her hands in delight. It had been hours since she'd eaten at the diner. Selecting a family size lasagna, Cassia unwrapped it and popped it in the microwave. Further digging in the cupboards revealed a single-serve coffee maker and hot chocolate inserts for the little machine. She made a huge cup of cocoa using two hot chocolate packets and sipped on it while her dinner cooked.

Once the microwave dinged, she grabbed the now cooked dinner and a fork and sat down at the counter to enjoy her first meal in her new house.

A distant banging woke Cassia from a deep sleep. What could be going on in the middle of the night? She pried her eyes open and rubbed the sleep out of them, looking around the room in confusion. She was in one of the guest bedrooms in the back of the main level, with the thick cream curtains pulled tightly shut. The curtains were three layers deep and had taken some muscle to get them shut the previous night. At least one room in this house had had curtains. She didn't know if she would have been able to sleep without that.

The room itself was cozy. Someone had invested a lot of money in expensively outfitting the four-poster walnut bed that dominated the room. A thick matelassé cover hid two blankets, including a wool one, and the most decadent sheets she'd ever slept on. Perhaps this was where all the money went, instead of new siding for the house, or heat even.

Two nightstands, a matching vanity and stool, as well as an armchair were the only other furniture. It was sparse, but at least it was not up the dark stairs. Exploring a house in the middle of the night had not been on Cassia's to-do list.

Plus, it had an attached bathroom. No running around in the middle of the night for her.

The warmth of the bed lulled Cassia's eyes back shut until the banging started up again. "All right, all right, I'm coming," Cassia said, throwing back the thick covers and getting out of bed. She shuffled to the window and pulled back the curtain on one side, recoiling at the brilliant sunshine that flooded the room.

Apparently it wasn't the middle of the night. Those were some amazing blackout curtains.

Miss Mansfield complained from the bed as the light hit her.

"What? Aren't you guys supposed to love sunshine?" Cassia asked.

Miss Mansfield meowed, then stood and stretched, sticking her furry rear in the air.

The banging got louder, as if whoever was at the door was getting impatient.

"I am not a morning person, and this is not helping," Cassia muttered as she looked around for her sweater and jeans. She'd been too tired last night to look for the suitcase with her pajamas, so had just slept in her underwear. Maybe not the smartest choice in a creepy old house. Add that to the task list: find pajamas, get curtains.

Cassia trudged through the house to the front door. The stained-glass window revealed the outline of a smaller person with spiky hair. Relieved that it looked like a woman, Cassia risked getting close enough to peer through the peephole. Outside, Genevieve peered back up at her, one eyeball scarily close to the lens of the peephole. It looked like a ridiculous panel from a Manga cartoon. Cassia jumped back from the peephole and shook herself.

After some fumbling with the lock on the heavy brass handle, Cassia pulled the door open. It gave way with an ominous creak.

Genevieve gave her a tentative smile and held up a basket. "Good morning." She wore narrow black pants, some kicking boots, and a stylish knit gray tunic. It was completely different from the silly blue fifties uniform she'd had on in the diner. She looked really good—and fashionable.

Cassia tugged her sweater down. Now she really wished she'd dug through her luggage for something better to wear.

"Good morning," Cassia said warily. She hadn't forgotten Genevieve's cold shoulder and strange behavior from yesterday. "Can I help you?"

"Aww, you're mad," Genevieve said and looked away for a moment, shifting uncomfortably before facing Cassia again. "Look, I don't blame you. I'm sorry about yesterday. I was just surprised."

"Why? I mean, you had to know someone was going to get the place," Cassia asked.

Genevieve's face flushed. "Actually, we thought it was going to be sold. We didn't think the old lady had any relatives."

"Tight-knit town, huh?" Cassia asked, folding her arms. "The way you interrogated me yesterday, I would've thought you knew everything about her."

"Yeah, I'm sorry about that, too. I was just so excited to see another person my age." Genevieve raised the basket again and held it out to Cassia. "I brought a peace offering."

Cassia narrowed her eyes at the basket, refusing to take it. "What?"

"Muffins, homemade," Genevieve said in a singsong voice. "And fresh coffee. As in the beans were roasted yesterday and ground today." She wagged her eyebrows.

Cassia bit her lips to keep from smiling.

"The same person who made your lunch yesterday prepared it all..." Genevieve said with more of the singsong tone while gently swinging the basket like a cat toy in front of her.

That delicious lunch. Cat's stomach rumbled.

"Oh, okay, come in," Cat said, trying to be brusque, but having to turn away before Genevieve saw her smile.

CHAPTER 5

Genevieve followed Cassia back through the house to the kitchen but didn't quite keep up. Cassia turned around to check on her and found the girl staring into several of the rooms that branched off the long hallway as they passed through it on their way to the kitchen near the back of the house. Her mouth hung open much the same way Cassia was sure hers had the day before.

The house was impressive, even just the one floor Sarah had had time to show her, but especially the two middle rooms Genevieve was looking at. The room on the west side was an enormous long library the size of two living rooms, with more books than Cassia thought most small towns had. Fitting in with the light wood of the decor, it had light birch bookshelves covering the walls, reaching right up to the ceiling. The architect had cleverly made this room two stories tall, right down to having the two enormous windows run from floor to ceiling on the far wall, letting in an impressive amount of light. Two old-fashioned ladders that ran on rails mounted to the front of the bookshelves on either side of the room made sure all the books were accessible.

Cassia was dying to see if there were some fancy astronomy books in there. Antique volumes were worth a fortune. She doubted Sarah the housekeeper would have any inkling of their value.

The room on the other side of the hallway was what Sarah had called a lady's parlor. It jutted out into the garden, or what had been the garden a few decades ago, with windows on three sides. It must have been magnificent at one time. Now dead ivy hung in front of the windows, giving it a bit of a gruesome look, incongruous with the fine linen furniture that filled the room. Cassia imagined some lady having her sewing circle in there, or tea, or whatever it was fine ladies did a century ago.

"You've never been inside the house?" Cassia asked.

Genevieve gave an embarrassed look and hurried to catch up with Cassia. "No, never."

"What about all those parties?" Cassia asked. "Sarah told me all about them."

Genevieve gave a tilt of her head.

"Sarah, the housekeeper..." Cassia prompted.

"Uh, townsfolk were never invited to those parties, at least that's what I've heard. Besides, that was a long time ago."

They entered the kitchen and Genevieve looked around in awe. Seeing Cassia's stare, she recovered herself and swung the basket onto the island, flipped open the lid and started unpacking it. The smell of hot blueberries and walnuts rolled over Cassia like a bulldozer. Seconds later, the crisp scent of a dark roast coffee followed when Genevieve unscrewed a huge metal thermos. Without asking, Genevieve dug in the cabinets and pulled out two ceramic mugs.

"Oh, wow. Can you come every day?" Cassia asked as she took the cup that Genevieve had poured for her. Blowing on the steaming black liquid, she took a sip. Oh for heavenly.

Cassia sat down at the island, watched Genevieve dig around in the cabinets and pull out some silverware and dishes.

"I don't think I have any butter," Cassia said.

Genevieve waved her off. "I brought everything. Even eggs in case you didn't eat muffins."

"You're completely forgiven, Genevieve," Cassia said with a smile.

"I do have one more thing to ask," Genevieve said, teasing Cassia as she sat down across from her and pushed over a plate and cutlery. "I don't know your name. With all the questions I asked, I never asked who you were."

Cassia reached out a hand over the island. "Cassia Lemon. Nice to meet you."

Genevieve took it and gave a firm shake. "Nice to meet you, Cassia Lemon."

"Cat, please," Cassia said. As if on cue, Miss Mansfield walked in, announcing herself with a meow.

Genevieve gave Cassia a questioning look.

"No, that," Cassia motioned to the cat, "is Miss Mansfield. I am Cat. A very unfortunate coincidence. She came with the house. Or maybe the house came with her, as I'm beginning to learn about cats."

"Ah, she's a beaut," Genevieve said.

Cassia made quick work of feeding Miss Mansfield and gave her a good head rub, and then sat back down.

Once Cassia returned, Genevieve grabbed a muffin and a tub of butter out of the basket, then shoved the basket to Cassia. Genevieve sliced open her muffin on her plate and put what must have been a quarter of a stick of butter on it. She motioned for Cassia to serve herself, then noticed Cassia's amazed look.

"What? The butter is better for you than the muffin is," Genevieve said with a laugh.

This was definitely her type of friend. Cassia put just as much butter on her muffin.

They ate for a few moments in silence. Cassia appreciated the time to wake up a bit more.

"So, you're not named Mandress," Genevieve said.

"No," Cassia said. "I didn't even know I had relatives with that name until the letter from the lawyer came."

"That explains it."

Cat narrowed her eyes at Genevieve, then relaxed and sat back in her chair and waved her hand. "I get it. You guys did an internet search thing."

"We did. No living Mandress anywhere in the country."

"Really?" Cassia asked, raising her eyebrows. "You guys were that interested? And who is we?"

A red flush rose over Genevieve's face. "Well, the town really. We were all gonna come through when the realtor did the open house. All three generations of the Smiths were good to come through and make a party of it afterwards. They already promised to invite us all."

"Why?" Cassia asked, shocked.

"Because no one is ever allowed in here. Not in like fifty years or something. This is like three normal houses. No, I'm exaggerating, more like five. It's freaking cool," Genevieve said, motioning to the house around them.

"It is pretty cool," Cassia admitted. She looked shyly at Genevieve. "I haven't even explored most of it. Yesterday was a long day."

"Sorry—"

"No, not you, or not *just* you guys. This place was rather a shock. And then I get yelled at for leaving my truck in the middle of my own driveway," Cassia said with a huff.

Genevieve covered her mouth to stifle a giggle. "Let me guess, Sheriff Andrews?"

"Yes," Cassia said, restraining herself from grimacing. "Charming man."

"Oh definitely, very charming," Genevieve said.

Cassia squinted at Genevieve. "Are you saying that ironically?"

"Oh definitely," Genevieve said and then burst out laughing. Cassia had to join in.

"Who styles that man?" Cassia asked, wiping her eyes, then standing to pick up her dish to put it in the sink. "Because he definitely looks styled."

"He lives alone as far as I know," Genevieve said.

"Well, if anyone would know, it's probably you." Cassia grabbed Genevieve's dish and put in the sink on top of hers, and then unscrewed the thermos and topped off both their cups.

"Maybe he just wanted to see the house too," Genevieve offered.

Oh boy. Was she going to have visitors all day long from these busybodies trying to peek inside the windows? Was that the only reason Genevieve was there?

As if reading her mind, Genevieve motioned to the house. "Yes, I'm curious, but more than that, I was excited to meet someone my age. Most of the people I went to high school with went off to college and never came back. Or if they did, they got married right away and have three kids already, or something like that."

"Three kids?" Cassia asked, incredulous. She could barely take care of herself. Who would have three kids already by their early twenties?

"Winters are really long here," Genevieve said by way of explanation.

"Ugh."

Genevieve nodded in agreement.

The muffin and coffee had put Cassia in a really good mood, not to mention having a friend to talk to, a girlfriend at that. "Well, you came all the way out here. You want to see some of the place?"

Genevieve's face lit up. "Do I ever."

Cassia waved her to follow.

———

They had already gone through the kitchen, the back bedrooms, the library and both of the front parlors off the main entryway when Cassia and Genevieve paused before the stairs leading to the second floor. The curving double staircase of birch wood covered with thick carpet runner of rose colored carpeting met above them in a small landing above and across from the entryway. Hallways ran off the landing to both the left and the right out of sight, to what Cassia presumed was the rest of the house, including more stairs to the third floor that were not visible here.

It looked like something right out of a glamorous 1920s movie. If the decor had been darker, it would have easily looked like something right out of a castle.

"What's up there?" Genevieve asked.

"I'm not sure," Cassia said.

"What do you mean you're not sure, isn't this your house?" Genevieve asked, not doing a good job of hiding her surprise.

"Well, I did just get here yesterday," Cassia said. She wasn't sure why she was making excuses. It did seem kind of silly that she didn't know. "Sarah said she'd show me today when she got here."

"Are there any locked rooms she told you not to go into too?" Genevieve asked, a smirk on her face.

Cassia stared at her for a moment, parsing the reference before she finally got it.

"You mean like Bluebeard?" Cassia asked. "No, not exactly."

"Not exactly? But there might be," Genevieve said, clearly teasing.

"Stop that," Cassia said. "This isn't a fairytale. Besides, I was more interested in getting sleep last night than wandering around a huge house by myself after dark."

"Fair enough," Genevieve said. "It is huge. I don't think I want to go wandering around too much after dark myself."

Cassia chewed her lip, thinking for a moment. "How about this, we go explore upstairs after I show you the coolest part of the main floor? Absolutely the coolest," Cassia said.

Genevieve's eyebrows rose. "Deal."

Cassia led her back through the long hallway, into the kitchen, and through it to the rear hall that led to the addition with the observatory in it. She flipped on the lights by the doorway and then opened the control panel to control the motors to open the dome. The light bulbs within the observatory were dim by design, so to get any real light inside the metal dome would have to be slid back in its wedge sections.

Genevieve walked into the room and looked around in awe. "What is this?"

"A really, really old telescope. It's probably more antique than useful, but it's still something amazing to have in your house," Cassia said with her back to Genevieve as she fumbled with the controls. She flicked the switch that she'd seen Sarah use yesterday to slide open the dome, but now only a few clicks from the dome sounded and then a humming noise came from the motor that was built into the wall below it. She turned it on and off with the same result. Fearing she was going to break the motor, Cassia turned it to the off position and then looked into the room with her hands on her hips. "I don't understand. It worked yesterday."

"Maybe there's something jammed in it," Genevieve said. "That's what old man Thompson's gate sounds like when he's trying to open it with something blocking it."

"You mean like a bird?" Cassia asked.

"Or a branch," Genevieve suggested. "We did have a storm last night."

They had? Wow, Cassia must've slept really soundly last night because she hadn't heard anything, much less a storm that would have brought down tree branches.

Cassia walked to the door in the back of the observatory that led to the outside. It was locked with the deadbolt. Cassia pulled the slender ring of keys Sarah had given her the night before from her pants pocket. None of the keys fit. Now that was irritating. Why didn't she have all the keys? Genevieve's words of locked rooms came back to her. A nauseous feeling congealed in her stomach.

No, no jumping to conclusions. Cassia gave Genevieve a weak smile and motioned for her to follow her into the kitchen.

It was as she remembered. The kitchen door that led to the garden locked with a handle lock. Even if she didn't have the correct key, she could unlock the door from the inside. Flipping the small lock tab, Cassia opened the door to the backyard and then stood in the doorway, hesitating.

What at one time had been a beautiful pathway now lay buried under knee-high grass, broken twigs, and dried looking bushes pushing their way in from all sides. No one had probably walked back here in years, decades even. Genevieve peered over Cassia's shoulder and gave a low whistle.

"Saving a ton of money on landscaping around here," Genevieve said.

Cassia nodded. "Wait for minute. I need to grab my shoes." Genevieve already had her shoes on, having not taken them off when she entered the house earlier.

Cassia ran through the house, scooped up her white tennis shoes from the pad by the front door and made it back to the back door in record time, but it wasn't fast enough. As Cassia thought she might, Genevieve couldn't help herself and was already out the back door exploring the backyard.

"Wait, wait," Cassia said, calling out the back door as she slipped on her tennis shoes and shoved the laces inside, not bothering to tie them. She didn't know if it was because she wanted to be first, or because she didn't want to be left behind in this house. Or maybe it was a little of both.

Standing near the back of the yard, Genevieve turned to face Cassia and gave her a huge smile. Cassia ran out the door, bounding through the tall grass and trying to avoid the bushes. She had spied huge thorns on one of the dried looking things, most of the barbs being at least an inch long, and she had no desire to rip holes in her best pair of jeans.

"Not going anywhere," Genevieve said, reassuring her. "At least not far."

They reached the end of the long yard together, and pushed through the scrawny branches of several lilac trees to turn the corner of the house to face the extension stuck off to one side, the one with the dome and the observatory built into it.

Cassia stopped walking abruptly as soon as they saw the dome. Genevieve, distracted with a loose thread on her tunic, looked up to see what had grabbed Cassia's attention.

"Holy moly, girl. What have you done?"

Cassia turned wide eyes to Genevieve. "What? What have I done?"

"Well you were here all night..." Genevieve said, trailing off at Cassia's incredulous expression.

They both turned back to look at the dome. Sprawling across it, and looking like he was hanging by a scarf around his neck that was looped on the top spire of the dome, was a young man. Or at least the body of a young man. Cassia had never seen a living person with the face that color blue before.

Cassia ran to the nearest bush and threw up.

The sound of her gagging bounced weirdly off the woods and the back of the house.

After a moment, Genevieve said, "I guess we should call the sheriff."

Cassia nodded from the bush, regretting her large breakfast.

CHAPTER 6

Cassia and Genevieve sat gloomily on the front stoop of the mansion. Several sheriff's cars parked at odd angles on the dead grass of the front lawn. At least they weren't blocking the driveway, Cassia thought as she picked up a stone and threw it away from the house.

The sun was high overhead and yesterday's chill gone. Cassia sweated under her sweater but didn't dare take it off because she had not yet had a shower that day. Genevieve didn't seem bothered by the warmth at all, her legs stretched out and leaning back to absorb as much of it as possible.

After Genevieve had been brave enough to run to the body and touch its leg to make sure the man was not still alive, they had run back into the house and called the sheriff. Sheriff Andrews had been out in minutes, which Cassia thought was weird considering how far out the house was. Finally satisfied they did not know anything about how the body got there, he ordered them to wait out front for further questioning.

Another much younger sheriff, looking more like a puppy dog than a man of the law with his chubby face and fuzzy brown hair, stood watch over them. He looked at them apologetically, but did not move from his spot twenty feet away.

Genevieve wasn't even going to work that day, something that was going to make a lot of people unhappy, apparently. There were only a few waitresses in Forgotten Valley. Cassia could hear the yelling of the hostess from several feet away as Genevieve tried to talk quietly with her on her cell phone.

Cassia kept checking the driveway, looking for Sarah's car. She wasn't even sure what it looked like, having not watched Sarah leave the previous night. The car must have been tucked away in some garage on the far side of the house. Not only had Cassia forgotten to get Sarah's cell phone number, she'd forgotten to ask about a schedule. Cassia had assumed she'd be out in the morning, but it was nearly noon and there was no sign of the woman.

A long white van came up the driveway, followed by a pickup truck with several ladders on the top. A man came out of the white van, draped head to toe in a paper covering—the sort that you see in disaster scenes. He looked questioningly at Genevieve and Cassia and they pointed to the rear of the house. He nodded and walked back, followed by a tall man wearing paint spattered overalls and an enormous straw hat who had come from the pickup truck and carried a gigantic ladder on his shoulders.

"Morning, Genevieve," the man with the ladder said.

"Morning, Roger," Genevieve said.

Genevieve caught Cassia's questioning look. "We only have one handyman..."

"... in Forgotten Valley," Cassia finished with her.

Cassia did not envy their task of getting the dead body down from the dome of the observatory. Her stomach cramped at the thought. She forced herself to focus on the overgrown weeds next to the stairs.

Sheriff Andrews came round the side of the house, walking

toward them with unmistakable purpose and a stern look on his face. Cassia imagined he thought this was all her fault and she brought trouble with her along with her parking-in-the-wrong-spot big city bad vibes.

Then he opened his mouth and confirmed it.

"Okay, Miss Lemon, we're going to have to check the inside of the house," he said.

"What?" Cassia asked, looking back at the house and feeling a bit of panic. "Why do you have to go inside? The man was out here, and the doors were locked all night."

"So you say," Sheriff Andrews answered, folding his arms across his chest and staring at Cassia. His shirt was so tight she thought his massive arm muscles might actually rip the shirt right in front of her. He really needed to buy a larger size. Or work out less.

"Yes, so I say." Cassia rose to her feet, brushing off her pants. Her hands shook. She shoved them in her pockets to try to stop them.

"This is a crime scene," Sheriff Andrews said slowly.

"Are you sure?" Cassia asked.

Genevieve rounded her eyes at Cassia.

"Maybe he just decided to kill himself there. Or it was an accident," Cassia's voice squeaked.

"He just decided to take a joyride on the roof of your house in the middle of nowhere and just happened to slip and fall to his death?" Sheriff Andrews said, sarcasm dripping from every word.

"Maybe?" Cassia said. "You don't know. I don't know. His scarf was caught on the spire on the top of the dome. It could have been an accident."

"I'm an officer of the law. I'm pretty sure I do know," Sheriff Andrews said.

"What?" Cassia asked.

"What what?" Sheriff Andrews said. His face was turning an interesting shade of red.

"You said you're pretty sure you know. What do you know?" Cassia asked. She knew she was digging a hole. Sure, why not, keep going. Soon she could jump right in and take the shovel in with her. Mother had always said she didn't have much horse sense, whatever that meant.

"That this is a crime scene!" Sheriff Andrews said, his voice ringing out in the courtyard. Roger peeked around the corner and quickly disappeared again when the second deputy waved him away.

"No," Cassia said.

"Cassia—" Genevieve said, stopping when Cassia raised a hand.

"I think you need a warrant. No. I know you need a warrant," Cassia said, facing off Sheriff Andrews. She didn't know why her gut instinct was to keep him out of the house, but considering not even she had been upstairs yet, she wanted a chance to look around before the sheriff and his crew were tripping around her house. And get the rest of the keys from Sarah. She didn't have the key to the observatory door. What other keys was she missing?

"Miss Lemon. You are obstructing justice," Sheriff Andrews said.

"I am not. I'm asking for warrant, which is something I am reasonably allowed," Cassia said. She straightened her arms, pushing her hands further into her pockets, mentally willing them to stop shaking.

Sheriff Andrews took a long moment to stare at her, then glanced up at the house, carefully checking each window. Cassia forced herself not to turn to see what he was seeing. "Fine, you'll have your warrant. Do not go anywhere. I expect you to still be here when I return in an hour." He poked his finger at her, emphasizing each word.

Cassia nodded numbly. She didn't think she was capable of driving at the moment anyhow.

Where was that Sarah?

The sheriff peeled out, his car leaving a trail of kicked up dust behind him, barely slowing as he hit the patch of road twisting through the trees. Even as traumatized as Cassia was, she still had to marvel at his amazing driving ability.

"What was that all about?" Genevieve asked Cassia quietly, angling her face away from the other sheriff eyeing them speculatively.

"I think they should follow the law," Cassia said defensively. She didn't know how much she should confide in Genevieve. They really only become friends, if they were friends, this morning.

———

She walked into the house, followed by Genevieve. They both stared up at the landing at the top of the double staircase. The early afternoon sun came in through the high windows over the doorway and hit the rose colored carpet runners on the stairs, giving a homey glow to the whole entrance. It seemed so warm and normal compared to the horror they had just seen outside.

Had she really heard nothing last night? Cassia couldn't even remember a single dream, much less hearing anything strange in the house. That itself was rather weird, considering she usually didn't sleep very well her first night in a new place.

Cassia thought for a minute, tapping her lips with her forefinger. Something in the left parlor window caught her eye. Outside, Roger, now also draped in the same emergency paper uniform as the first guy from the long van, was helping the van guy carry out a stretcher with a full body bag on it.

Genevieve stared. "That was quick work."

"Are you sure you didn't know that guy? The one that died." Cassia asked.

Genevieve shook her head. "No. He looked about our age and I would've known anyone like that, at least anyone who'd grown up here."

"So it was a stranger," Cassia said. "Did most people who came to the mansion come through town? I mean, you didn't seem to know much about Sarah."

"I thought everyone came through town, but yeah," Genevieve acknowledged, "apparently there is some back way to get here."

Cassia gazed around the mansion, trying to piece together her thoughts. "Did you know that this mansion is not on any mapping software I tried?"

"Oh, Mildred Mandress was proud of that one. Once or twice a year, she'd come in to town to eat at the diner, and woe to anyone who complained about that to her. 'You don't need to come out there anyway. It's not a public zoo for your rug rats to come visit.'" Genevieve imitated a high-pitched nasal voice. "And those were some of the nicer things she said."

Cassia wanted to laugh. Maybe she had inherited some of her bluntness from Aunt Mildred. Would she be that crotchety when she was seventy-five years old? Sheriff Andrews would probably say yes.

The door swung open and Sarah entered in a rush, nearly knocking Cassia and Genevieve over. Today she wore a violet skirt suit with a matching pill box hat. She was a fashion plate from about seventy years ago. It looked weird on a woman so young.

"Who—?" Sarah asked, looking at Genevieve and taking a step back at the unexpected presence in the house.

"Sarah, this is Genevieve. She's from the diner downtown. She brought muffins," Cassia said, realizing she was prattling.

"Did she bring the sheriff, too?"

"No, uhm..." Cassia searched for the words.

"We found a dead body in the back," Genevieve blurted out. Cassia stared at her. Perhaps she was also related to Aunt Mildred.

"You what?" Sarah asked, looking back and forth between the two of them. "Where? Is that why sheriff junior didn't want me to come in here. Luckily, I walked faster than he does."

Cassia turned to the window by the front door. Sure enough, the second sheriff was on the stoop looking in. Sheriff Junior wasn't a bad name for him, she had to admit. Cassia opened the door.

"It's okay, she works here," Cassia said to the sheriff. He did not look happy, shifting from foot to foot, but merely nodded and turned his back to the door.

After a second, he turned back again. "She can't leave, because Sheriff Andrews—"

"—wants everyone to stay. Got it," Cassia finished for him, then shut the door.

"Stay? For how long?" Sarah asked.

"Until they're done questioning us, I guess," Cassia said, a bit of bitterness in her voice. This inheriting a mansion thing was not turning out at all.

"That won't work..." Sarah said, then trailed off, staring off into space as if thinking of something else.

Cassia narrowed her eyes at her. She just got there. "Did you know I don't have all the keys?"

"What?" Sarah asked, distractedly.

Cassia sidestepped so she was standing in front of Sarah. "The keys to the house. I don't have them all."

Sarah's eyes slowly focused on Cassia. "Oh, sorry. I must've given you the wrong key ring. I'm sure it's around here somewhere."

Sarah put her oversized matching violet purse on one of

the wooden chairs pushed up against the walls in the entryway, then dug through it. "Not in here. Probably in the kitchen."

"Aren't you curious about the body?" Cassia asked as Sarah was about to walk off to the kitchen. Sarah turned around slowly.

"That's a little macabre isn't it?" Sarah asked.

"It was a person, that was alive, and now they're not. And it happened here. I just thought… You might be curious. You wouldn't happen to know a young man about our age who likes to wear scarves?" Cassia asked.

"No, absolutely not," Sarah answered so fast that Cassia barely had time to finish the question.

"You don't know any young man?" Cassia asked.

Sarah drew herself up tall, and looked down her nose at Cassia, her sunny disposition disappearing faster than Cassia could say apple sauce. "Miss Lemon, this is my place of business. I work here. I don't bring any personal business here. Certainly, I would never, ever, bring another person here. I take my job very seriously. I do not appreciate you questioning my morals or my word. Am I clear?"

A chill ran down Cassia's back. She did not like this new side of Sarah. What happened to the friendly woman of yesterday? "Yes, I think we're clear on this."

Sarah turned and walked briskly to the kitchen, her heels clicking on the floor.

"Whoa, she works for you?" Genevieve asked. "You sure about that?"

Heat flared on Cassia's face. "Supposedly."

"Meow."

Genevieve and Cassia looked up to see Miss Mansfield delicately walking across the landing above them. When the tiny black cat saw them looking at her, she gave a sassy flick of her tail, and then ran off down the hallway to the left out of sight.

Genevieve and Cassia looked at each other.

"Maybe she's trying to tell us something," Genevieve said.

Cassia thought for about one second about telling Sarah they were going upstairs without her, and then dismissed it. She wasn't in the mood for more of what had just happened.

"I think she might be," Cassia said. They both ran up the stairs, trying to stay on the runner and be as quiet as possible, while still making good enough speed to not lose the cat.

The left hallway ran half the width of the house, with a huge window at the end and several doors coming off on each side. All the doors were shut. At the far end, by the window, the open space to the right gave Cassia the impression of another stairwell. That must be how one reached the third floor.

Miss Mansfield was nowhere in sight. When Cassia and Genevieve stopped running, the only thing Cassia could hear was her own labored breathing. The wall to wall rose carpeting in the hallway muffled any noise in the hallway. Suddenly, Cassia felt like she had to whisper.

"Did you see where she went?" Cassia asked.

Genevieve shook her head.

They walked down the hallway, the carpet crushing under their feet as the pad below it gave way. It had the subtle sheen of new carpet. Cassia had never been able to afford an apartment with new carpet, much less a house. Why had the Mandresses spent money on that but let the outside of the house rot on its frame?

Cassia walked over to the nearest door on the left and tried it. The handle didn't budge. Locked. Not only was the handle locked, a hole for a key showed below the handle. Cassia was sure that was locked, too.

Genevieve's eyebrows rose as she watched Cassia try the door. "Why would someone lock the doors on an empty house?"

"I was thinking the same thing," Cassia said. Maybe she

shouldn't be exploring the house with Genevieve, but it just felt so good to have someone else with her.

A call from below signaled Sarah had come back to the entryway and found them missing.

Cassia held up a finger to her lips to signal quiet and then waved for Genevieve to follow her to the end of the hall, where a stairway did indeed rise up another floor. The cat must have gone up there.

The stairway was half the width of the hallway, but it had carpet from edge to edge of the steps. It felt intimate and cozy, unlike the scale of the rest of the house that felt more like a museum than a home. It twisted three times, rising higher than Cassia would have expected, and ended in a narrow door set slightly open. The doorframe was damaged around the lock and fresh white wood splinters showed where the stained wood had split.

Cassia and Genevieve slowed to a halt. The damage looked recent.

A faint meow from inside the room rang out and then abruptly cut off with a squeak. Cassia's stomach flipped and her heart raced. She glanced out the window in the stairwell that looked out into the yard. They were at least thirty feet above any help on the outside below them.

CHAPTER 7

Cassia gripped the polished wooden handrail tightly. Genevieve was doing the same on her side of the stairway. They stood, frozen in place on the carpeted stairwell, waiting to hear another meow—or any noise, actually—from inside the room just above them. The entrance curved to their left, so nothing was visible in the cracked doorway except for a plain white wall ahead. No hint of what lay beyond in the room at the top of the stairs visible.

Below, and outside, faint voices spoke of those below cleaning up the scene where the body had been found that morning. Cassia thought the van with the body must be gone, so other detectives and people from the sheriff's office must be below. They seemed like a mile away, for all the good they would do if Cassia and Genevieve needed help. Suddenly, coming up the stairs by themselves seemed like a really poor idea.

Cassia shut her eyes for a moment, then opened them again, determined. They were there now, and there were two of them.

Besides, Miss Mansfield had not seemed concerned.

But then again, maybe she should not be taking her behavioral clues from a cat.

Cassia looked to Genevieve, who nodded back. The determined look on Genevieve's face said she was thinking the same thing about going into the room. They had to do it.

Cassia held up one hand, then extended one finger, then a second, then a third, and then motioned for them to go.

Cassia and Genevieve scrambled up the stairs and ran into the room.

No one was in it.

The room was a small square, with a desk in the center, a wooden library chair on wheels behind it, and low shelves all around the room. Papers covered all the surfaces and spilled off the desk onto the floor.

A window on the far side stood open. There was no screen.

"No cat," Genevieve said after making a cursory attempt to check under some of the piles of paper. Cassia doubted the fussy feline would have tolerated being in such places anyway.

Cassia walked to the window and looked out. About ten feet below and toward the main house, the roof curved in a gentle slope toward the backyard. This room was actually higher than the third floor and looked out something like a tower. Over the roof line, she could see people walking in the backyard. More official looking people in those white paper suits.

The dome of the observatory was visible from the window as well. The spiky brass spire that marked the center of the dome, and where each segment of the dome's leafs rotated around, shone in the sunlight. A ragged bit of scarf still clung to the spire, but the body was gone. A streak of clean brass marked where it had been dragged down one of the dome's sections, rubbing off the dirt there.

"Where did she go?" Cassia asked, wondering if they had somehow missed the cat, Miss Mansfield, in their rush to the end of the hallway.

Genevieve joined her at the window, looking out, then grabbed the sill to steady herself as she leaned out to peer left and right. The roof below extended a little past where they were and behind them, wrapping around the tower and as far as the stairwell behind them. "Huh. I don't know."

"You heard her, right?" Cassia asked. "The cat. I mean, it sounded like she was right up here."

"Ah, yeah, I would say," Genevieve said. She stood back up and wiped the dirt from her tunic and pants. The windowsill and the wall below it were filthy with red brown dirt. Chunks of the dirt lay in small piles on the floor, and on some of the papers, smearing red stains on them.

Another meow came, this time from much farther away, or so it seemed. It was from outside the window; Cassia was sure of that. She stood at the sill, determined to find the cat.

Finally, the curl of a black tail showed against the blue sky as Miss Mansfield delicately walked along the roofline closer to the dome. She stood on the roof just above where the second story addition joined the house. Cassia pointed her out to Genevieve.

"Well, that is one mystery solved," Cassia said.

"Funny place to take a walk," Genevieve said.

"That it is," Cassia said, looking around the room. Besides the dirt, the room looked dry and well taken care of, despite the mess of papers everywhere. She doubted the window was left open for the cat to make its excursions outside on a regular basis. Water would have ruined everything in here with the first rainstorm.

"What is all this stuff?" Genevieve asked. She picked up a piece of paper. One side was blank, and the other was filled with text.

Cassia picked up a piece of paper to examine herself. The text looked like gibberish. No, wait, it was that fake placeholder text stuff they use on document templates. Ipso something. "This is garbage."

"And there is a lot of it," Genevieve said, looking around the room. She picked up a few pieces from other piles and from the papers that had slipped to the floor. It was all the same. "Who would bother to print all the stuff out?"

Cassia rubbed her head. Nothing in this house made sense. This day was getting worse and worse.

"Miss Lemon," an irritated female voice called from below. "Sheriff Andrews is back, and he wants to speak to you. Now, Miss Lemon!"

Sarah. Her voice rang in the hallway below. She must be walking the second floor trying to find her and Genevieve.

Cassia groaned. Sheriff Andrews must have his search warrant if he was back already. Time to get this over with.

———

Cassia and Sheriff Andrews sat in one of the front parlors. Cassia sat on the edge of her seat, uneasy to be on the light linen colored sofa still in her clothes from yesterday. Sheriff Andrews sat across from her in a huge armchair that looked like a gigantic yellow flower with his stern face as one of the stems coming out the middle. It was a ridiculous image.

Cassia had to admit she felt a little manic. This could not possibly be happening.

A thump by the front entryway reminded her that yes, indeed, it was really happening.

While they were sitting there for her interview, the front door stood open, allowing a steady stream of workers wearing white paper oversuits and carrying boxes of equipment in and out of the mansion. It seemed that Sheriff Andrews had returned with an entire army to go along with his search warrant to go through the place. They were not wasting any time and were going through every single floor room by room, judging by the thumps and bangs from overhead. Sarah's shrill voice rang out occasionally, scolding the workers when they carelessly banged into the walls or rattled at the doors too much while waiting for her to come unlock them.

Sheriff Andrews cleared his throat while scowling down at a notepad in front of him. A small voice recorder sat on the armchair of his chair, its microphone pointed at Cassia.

His badge and utility belt and stern expression did not fit in the genteel look of the room, with its delicate furniture and pastel mint walls. For that matter, neither did Cassia.

"Miss Lemon, are you sure you did not hear anything last night?" he asked.

"For the third time, I did not," Cassia said, instantly regretting the first part of her sentence when he looked up and scowled at her.

"This is a murder investigation," he said.

"Are you sure it was a murder? Is there something I should know?" Cassia asked. This was the time he stated that they were considering it a murder as a fact.

His eyes turned back down to the pad as he said in a quieter voice, "Most likely."

Cassia exhaled heavily, regretting that instantly as well. She had to go the bathroom, her throat was dry, and her butt hurt. As pretty as this couch was, it was not comfortable. Whoever bought it had been ripped off.

"We're going to need you to come down to the station and make a statement," he said.

"Why?" Cassia asked. She motioned to his pad and recorder. "Isn't that enough?"

He stood, and narrowed his eyes at her. From her angle on the couch he looked really tall.

"No, it's not. We're going to need you to sign something. You are our number one suspect," he said as he closed his notebook with a snap.

"What? I was inside. Sleeping," Cassia said. She gripped the cushion and held on tightly as the room around her seemed to be moving.

"So you say," Sheriff Andrews answered. "You come here one day, and the next there's a body. How do you think that looks?"

He turned and walked out of the room, leaving Cassia to stare after him with her mouth hanging open.

She stood and yelled after him, "Does that mean I need a lawyer?"

He turned the corner to go back to the kitchen without responding to her. One of the workers in a white paper suit and holding a huge equipment suitcase stared at her, then quickly scurried up the stairs away from her when she glared back at him.

Cassia ran to the hallway to catch Sheriff Andrews but turned the corner and walked directly into the second sheriff, Sheriff Junior, as Sarah had called him. He held up one hand to stop her.

"Ma'am, we're going to need you to not go back there for now," he said.

"This is my house! Mansion, whatever," Cassia said, mortified when her voice broke into a squeak.

"Nevertheless."

Cassia glared at him, and he dropped his eyes, but he did not budge from his spot. Nor did he lower his hand.

Cassia crossed her arms. She felt like a petulant six-year-old but could not stop herself.

They stood at a standoff for what felt like a full minute. Finally, Cassia dropped her arms.

"Fine, but my name is Cassia, Cassia Lemon. Please stop with the ma'am stuff. You are making me feel old," Cassia said.

He looked up at that and gave her a gentle understanding look. "All right, Miss Lemon. I am Deputy Chester, by the way."

"Is that a first name or last name?" Cassia asked.

He gave her a broad smile. "It is good that you still have a nice sense of humor with all that's going on," he said as he waved to the chaos in the mansion, then turned and walked after Sheriff Andrews.

"Wait," Cassia called after him, but he just chuckled and waved his hand as he walked, not even bothering to look back.

Had he not answered her question intentionally?

Cassia stood in the hallway, unsure what to do. Genevieve came down the hall, passing Deputy Chester. Her eyes red. Even her spiky black hair looked a little wilted.

"Are you okay?" Cassia asked.

"Yes, just a little freaked out," Genevieve said, avoiding Cassia's eyes and turning to dab at her nose with her sleeve. Cassia grabbed a tissue for her from a mother of pearl box on the table in the front hallway and handed it to her.

"About the body?" Cassia asked and felt like an idiot immediately afterwards. Probably, like duh? How often do you find a dead body?

Genevieve blew her nose surprisingly loud into the tissue and then nodded. "Yeah, that's it." She wiped away the tears from her eyes with the sleeve of her tunic and turned back to Cassia. "Do you have a lawyer?"

Cassia frowned. "No."

Genevieve gave an awkward laugh. "Well, I guess you won't have to worry about fixing the outside of the mansion if they take you away to jail." At Cassia's stricken look, she held up a hand. "I'm sorry. I've got a dark sense of humor. I'm sure it won't come to that. Especially since you're innocent. Sheriff

Andrews will probably just pull a power trip and try to keep you in jail for a week or two or three to make you confess."

Could he do that?

No, no, no.

Cassia definitely needed a lawyer.

CHAPTER 8

Dust moats twisted in the air, highlighted in the sunlight streaming in the huge pane of ancient glass in the storefront window of Forgotten Valley Lawyers, LTD. Huge gold lettering on the window showed the name written on the glass in a gigantic curve, like some emblem of honor.

The inside of the waiting room had dark carpeting, dark paneling, and dark wooden chairs covered with green leather and decorative brass tacks pinning the leather to the frame. Besides the half dozen uncomfortable chairs pushed up against the wall, there was only the large secretary's desk, a dark wood affair like everything else, and the secretary that went with it.

Cassia sat in one of the wooden chairs closest to the windows, her school backpack crushed into a pile on her lap. She kept looking out the windows to see who was walking around downtown Forgotten Valley, but it seemed strangely quiet.

The secretary looked up at Cassia and Cassia stopped fidgeting. The secretary was so old she looked like she had been around when the building was made in the twenties. Cassia tried not to stare at the woman when she wasn't staring out the window. The secretary was a tiny thing, with a full-on beehive hairdo nearly as big as she was, and was typing on an avocado green electric typewriter. The keys clicked rhythmically in the silence.

The secretary looked up and gave Cassia a gentle smile. "He will be with you shortly. Lunch hour is almost over."

A bell sounded from the next room over, much like a kitchen timer. It silenced abruptly. The secretary motioned for Cassia to enter the office adjoining the waiting room.

The office was the same dark motif as the waiting room, with an even larger desk that looked large enough to fill a conference room.

Except perhaps it might be the right size for the gentleman who was currently using it.

He stood and confirmed her suspicions. He held out a hand to shake hers, and she took it, having to crane upwards to look at his face. He must be close to seven feet tall. His dark hair was slicked back and parted neatly on the side. He wore a black suit and looked like nothing so much as a very dignified linebacker in his early fifties running a law firm. At least that is what the linebackers at the university had looked like, as her onetime boyfriend had smugly corrected her when she had called them quarterbacks.

"Thank you for waiting, Miss Lemon. My name is Nathaniel Perauski. You can call me Nate. I hear you've had some excitement," he said.

Cassia extracted her hand from his enormous one and tilted her head at him questioningly.

"You're surprised I know?" He gave a laugh. "This is a very small town. I think that will be one of your first lessons here." His look turned serious. "That is, if you get to spend much time here."

Cassia's heart sank and took her stomach with it down to her feet.

"That bad?" she blurted out, unable to help herself.

He motioned for her to sit, then slowly folded his enormous height down to sit behind his desk. "No, not necessarily, but we need to get to work quickly. I hear you have only been here for one day when they discovered the, ahem, body."

"Yes. Genevieve and I discovered him when I was showing her around the house yesterday. I'd only arrived the day before."

Nate opened a pen and pulled the pad toward himself. "Did you notice anything suspicious about the house when you arrived?"

Cassia shook her head.

"Did you go around the property and inspect it that first day? Especially the back, where you found him?"

Cassia shook her head again.

He looked up and raised an eyebrow.

"It was kind of late," Cassia said. "We, meaning Sarah and I, did open the dome where the kid was found. Or found on top of. I don't think the dome would have worked if he was hanging there that day."

"Why do you think that?" he asked.

"Because he sort of… jammed the motor. That's why we went outside, because I couldn't get it open."

"I see." He scribbled on the pad. "Did you notice anything else in the house?"

"Not really. I had only seen the first floor, anyway. And it turns out I didn't have most of the keys," Cassia said. It sounded really bad as she said it.

Nate put the pen down and leaned back. "You didn't have the keys?"

"Sarah hadn't given them to me yet. Or at least not all of them. Sarah, the housekeeper."

"I see. Is she looking for a lawyer too?" He asked, trying to make a joke of it, but Cassia didn't feel like laughing. He cleared his throat. "In all seriousness, she's not a suspect?"

"Not as far as I know, but it's not like Sheriff Andrews is telling me what's going on at all. I'm surprised they even allowed me to go back into my own house… mansion… whatever," Cassia said bitterly.

"I'm surprised you are too, actually," Nate said, his tone gentle. "Sheriff Andrews can be, shall we say, a little enthusiastic."

Yup, he knew the man.

"How did you get the mansion to begin with?" Nate asked, pulling his pad back to himself and leaning forward to get back to work.

"That's sort of a long and weird story, but since I'm here anyway, I did have some questions about this inheritance deal. I really didn't understand what the lawyers told me back in California, but I had to get out of town and didn't want to keep bothering them."

Cassia opened her backpack and pulled out a thick envelope. From the envelope she drew out a sheaf of folded papers, which she tried to lay out flat on his desk. Those papers had been the bane of her existence. No matter how many times she went over the tiny legalese writing, she still wasn't sure if she understood everything. What lawyer from the netherworlds had Aunt Mildred found to draw up this will? Finally giving up on smoothing them out, Cassia pushed the mass of paperwork to the lawyer.

He pulled them closer with one pinched forefinger and thumb. "The will, I take it," he said. He started reading the front page. "Your aunt?" he said, looking over the papers at Cassia.

She nodded.

"Were you close?" he asked.

"I didn't even know she existed," Cassia said.

"That explains a lot," he said, as his eyes dropped back down to the papers.

Cassia bit her lip so she wouldn't ask what that meant. Perhaps he, too, was going to go on the tour of the mansion and party afterwards at the Smiths. The whole town was probably invited. Maybe he was just as shocked as everyone else that there was a living relative.

Whatever. There was no sense in alienating her one hope right now when she was dealing with ridiculous murder charges. Or possible murder charges. Sheriff Andrews had only said, "We'll be in touch. Don't go anywhere."

Cassia shuddered.

"Interesting," Nate said to himself.

Cassia opened her mouth to ask a question, and without looking up, Nate held up one finger for her to not speak. Cassia scowled and grabbed the edge of the chair cushion to keep herself from fidgeting.

He flipped up one page, still engrossed in the document, and then another. A tiny clock on his desk clicked away the minutes. At his rates, it should just be making the sound of a cash register over and over again. That was money Cassia could not afford right now. She may have a house, but she didn't have much in the way of money, not just yet. As far as she could tell from the document, that was not something that would be released to her for at least a year, and even then, it wasn't really how clear how much she could expect.

She shifted uneasily in the hardback chair facing his desk. If he was going to charge that much per hour, he could at least give his clients a soft place to sit. There wasn't even a window to stare out of. Much as she appreciated having a lawyer to talk to, it felt excruciating to sit there in that dusty office in what could be one of her last days of freedom.

"It says here you have to live in the house for a year to

inherit it. It's in some sort of trust right now?" he asked, looking up from the document.

Cassia shrugged her shoulders. "You're the expert in legal mumbo jumbo."

He slid the will back onto the desk, then tented his fingers and stared at her contemplatively.

"What it says is, basically, that if you're gone for more than thirty days consecutively, or more than sixty days total, within the twelve month probationary period, you forfeit all claim to the house," he said.

"Can you say that a little simpler?" Cassia asked. If he had been talking about star trajectories or how much mass it took for a star to become a supernova, that would have been easy. Give her numbers any day, but this convoluted legal stuff made her head hurt.

"If they take you to jail for more than a month, you'll lose the mansion," he said.

"Wait, what?" she asked. "Wouldn't my legal address still be the mansion?"

"No, Miss Lemon. I'm not sure about what happens when they're holding you during a trial—I'll have to check on that—but if you're convicted and sent to prison, your official legal address is the prison."

"Not the mansion," Cassia said, her eyes wide.

"Not the mansion," he said, confirming. "Was there anyone that didn't want you to inherit this place?"

Probably the whole town, the thought raced through her head.

No. They wouldn't set her up just so they could have a tour of the place.

"Miss Lemon?" Nate asked. "Are you okay?"

Cassia realized she'd been staring at the wall behind him. "Yes, I'm fine. Well, I'm not fine, I have sort of a big problem, as you know." She slapped a hand over her own mouth to stop herself from prattling.

"Do you know of anyone who wanted the place?" he asked again.

Cassia shook her head. "Not that I know of."

"No relatives?"

"My parents." Cassia hesitated for a second. She hated saying it. It made it more real. "My parents are dead. So are my grandparents. My parents… when they were alive, they didn't really talk about family. I learned not to ask."

Heat rushed up over Cassia's face. It wasn't until she'd made friends in college that she learned just how weird that was. Most of her friends could recite their family trees to second and third cousins.

"So you don't know about any cousins or extended family?" he asked, his tone gentler this time.

Cassia shook her head again.

He nodded. "Okay then, we'll just have to do the best we can." Picking up the will with one hand, he motioned to her. "Can I make a copy of this?"

"You have a copy machine?" Cassia asked.

He tilted his head at her.

"You know, with the electric typewriter and all…" Cassia mumbled and pointed in the general direction of the secretary in the waiting room outside.

Nate laughed. "Ah, I see. Ms. Anderson prefers the electric, but we do have some newer technology around here." He leaned in close to her ear and whispered, "You wouldn't believe how hard it is to get help in this town."

Somehow Cassia thought she did.

Ten minutes later, Cassia had her copy of the will back and an appointment in two days to see the lawyer again if nothing else changed. He promised to research the conditions of the will and get back to her. Despite the reassurance of his help, somehow she felt worse than when she arrived.

If someone had committed a murder just to keep her out of the mansion, then they really didn't want her there.

A chill ran down Cassia's back. She pulled her jacket tight around herself as she opened the door to the blustery main street. She had to get some answers about the mansion and the people of this town, and fast.

CHAPTER 9

Cassia walked down the main street of Forgotten Valley. It was strangely empty, even for a Tuesday afternoon. Half of the storefronts she passed had signs over the front reading 'Closed, Please Come Back.'

The wind picked up, sending leaves hustling down the street. Cassia pulled up her hood over her green hat and zipped her jacket up as far as it would go. It wasn't even winter yet, and already she was freezing. It was even worse than Ted had promised. No wonder he was in California and no longer in the Midwest.

She let out an exhalation of relief when she got to the diner and saw the lights on inside. Pulling the door open, she entered with the ringing of bells and the bluster of wind and leaves coming in with her. The door shut behind her and the welcome warmth hit her face and fingers.

Only two people were in the diner—Genevieve and a young looking man with dark curly hair. He looked so much like one of Cassia's physics teaching assistants that she did a double take to make sure he wasn't.

Genevieve wore her funky blue diner uniform, but she

hunched over a cup at the counter, sitting on a stool next to the young man like she was off duty. He wore a chef's white shirt and a chef's cap sat on the counter next to him. He, too, had a cup of something warm.

"Where is everyone?" Cassia asked, pulling back her hood and taking off her hat.

"Apple Festival, one town over," Genevieve said, getting up and going around the back of the counter. "Coffee?"

Cassia nodded.

Genevieve motioned to the counter. "Come join us. It's a slow day. I, for one, am glad to not be out drinking cider and eating apple pie and brats."

Cassia raised her eyebrows as she sat down on the stool next to where Genevieve had been, and pulled close the steaming cup of coffee Genevieve poured for her. "That doesn't sound all that bad."

Genevieve laughed. "Okay, I'll take you someday. Meanwhile, we're here today and we have peace and quiet. Besides, today is only the preview anyhow, just for the surrounding towns. Next weekend is the full show for the tourists."

Cassia wrinkled her nose. "Crowds?"

"You betcha," Genevieve said in an exaggerated accent and gave Cassia a finger gun check of approval. "That's why the townsfolk like to have their own private event before they rake in all the tourist dollars with the big show."

Cassia looked over at the young man while Genevieve went to the pie display and cut a large slice and put it on a plate. "Hi," Cassia said to him, giving a little wave.

"Hi," he said. "I'm the chef here."

"And owner," Genevieve said over her shoulder as she grabbed another plate.

"And owner," he said with self-deprecation. He leaned into Cassia and offered his hand. "Trent Stevens."

His words finally sank into Cassia's frozen brain. "Oh my

gosh, you're the chef. You've made all the wonderful food I've eaten," she said.

"And what you're about to eat," he said with a wink as Genevieve slid a plate with pie in front of Cassia.

"You looked like you could use some sugar," Genevieve said as she grabbed the coffee pot and refilled her and Trent's cups.

Cassia picked up the fork and took a large bite of the apple pie encrusted with large grains of sugar. Heaven exploded in her mouth and pleasure rang through her body all the way down to her toes. The layers of the crust melted in her mouth. Cassia shut her eyes and concentrated on chewing. It shouldn't be possible for something to taste this good. After swallowing, she opened her eyes and looked over at Trent. "What are you doing here?"

He lifted his cup. "Well, at the moment, I'm having a cup of coffee," he said with a smirk.

"You know what I mean," Cassia said. "In this town. Your cooking is amazing. You could work anywhere."

He waved off her comment. "Yeah, yeah, yeah. I'm happy here for now."

"And we're happy with you here now too," Genevieve said, coming around the counter with her own piece of pie. She sat down between Trent and Cassia. "So, how was the lawyer?"

Cassia scowled. "Not great." At Genevieve's concerned look, she rushed on. "I mean, his lawyering is probably fine, but he couldn't exactly give me great news." Genevieve obviously already knew about the body, but Cassia didn't feel like talking about her possibly losing the mansion, especially in front of Trent, who she didn't know at all.

She didn't even want to think about it, honestly. Her life seemed to be on a disaster roll.

"How's it going at the house?" Genevieve asked when it was clear Cassia wasn't going talk anymore about the lawyer.

"Get a chance to explore the rest?" She said the question casually, but Cassia knew Genevieve was hanging on to the answer. She thought it strange Cassia didn't have all the keys.

Frankly, so did Cassia.

Cassia put her fork down on her plate and turned to face Genevieve and Trent directly. "No, I do not have all the keys. Still. And nearly all the rooms are locked again. Sarah keeps telling me she must've misplaced them and acts like it's all a mix-up, but she's so precise with the rest of her life, it just seems like…"

"An act?" Genevieve suggested.

"Yes. I'm starting to get really pissed off about it."

"It's your place, right?" Genevieve asked.

"Right?" Cassia asked. She turned back to the remnants of her pie and polished it off, pushed the plate and fork forward, and put her elbows on the table and rested her head in her hands. Speaking down to the gold flecked counter, she ranted off her complaints. "Sarah, who was always impeccably dressed, by the way, shows up sometime around noon—at least she has for two days in a row now—claims to not know where the keys are, yet could magically find them to let the sheriff's department crawl over the mansion, and locked up again after them, and now poof! The keys are magically gone again. All with a smile on her face and acting so friendly so I feel like an awful person for getting mad at her."

"Wow, that's some disrespect," Trent said. "Guessing she's not happy you're there. I wonder if she did that to old Mrs. Mandress?"

That was a good question. Nothing had been said in the will about a Sarah Rheton the housekeeper. It only mentioned 'staff.' Had she been the housekeeper when the will was written? Was there any way Cassia could find out? Another thing for her list of questions.

Genevieve licked her fork, then set it down on her plate and pushed it away as well. "What you need is a locksmith."

Cassia lifted her head. "Is there one in town?"

"Absolutely. Mandy. She's a great lady," Genevieve said. She grabbed a napkin and pulled a pen from her waitress apron pocket as well as her cell phone. Scrolling through the contacts, she finally found the one she was looking for and set the phone on the counter and began to copy the information onto the napkin. "She's probably gone to the festival today and won't be up for anything until tomorrow morning because she likes cider, a lot, but here's her number."

"You keep her number in your cell phone?" Cassia asked.

"Yeah," Genevieve said with a laugh, "I sorta lock myself out of my car often. She's pretty nice about it though and gives me the group discount for my big old group of one." She gave the napkin to Cassia, who glanced at it, then folded it and put it in her pocket.

"Too bad she's not available right now," Cassia said. "I just feel like Sheriff Andrews is going to come for me any day now." She gave Trent an embarrassed glance.

"Sarah's home now though, isn't she?" Genevieve asked. "Not sure I want to face her when bringing in a locksmith."

Cassia had to agree. "Sarah is there. She arrived just before I started up the van to come down here. Have to return that soon, by the way."

"Need a ride?" Genevieve asked.

Cassia nodded.

"I'm off tomorrow. Soon enough?"

"Yeah, I put extra time on the contract just in case I had problems on the road. That ought to work. Maybe I'll even see if there're some cars in that garage up at the mansion. That's locked, too. Of course."

Trent laughed into his coffee. "And I thought catering for that woman was tough," he said ruefully.

Cassia stared at him. "You've worked for her? For Sarah, I mean."

"Only once, when she first came on, I think. Mrs. Mandress had a cocktail party for her old friends or something like that. I'd never seen so many old ladies in my life. Old ladies who could drink." He shook his head at the memory.

"So Sarah's a new staff member?" Cassia asked. Genevieve seemed interested in the question, too.

"As far as I know. It was just a little while after I first got to town and hadn't bought the diner yet. One of my first stops in town had been going to the mansion to ask about any possible open personal chef positions. Some housekeeper who looked even older than Mrs. Mandress answered the door. She tried to shoo me away but the lady of the house caught her at it and insisted I come in for cookies because I was so cute." He ducked away as Genevieve tried to pinch his cheek. "They were quite the pair. I didn't realize at first that one was the lady and one was the housekeeper. I thought they were sisters," Trent said. He swirled the last of the coffee in his cup and then threw it back and set the cup aside. "A couple months later, I got a call about the party. There was no mistaking Sarah, or Mrs. Rheton as she insisted I call her, was in charge when I came to provide the food."

"When was that?" Cassia asked.

"Oh, probably two years ago or so. Right before I got this place," Trent said as he got up from his chair. "Nice to meet you. I've got some bookkeeping to take care of. Genevieve, lock up the front when you're done, okay? I think we're clear for the day."

"Will do, boss," Genevieve said. She turned to Cassia. "Want to do some more exploring tonight? Maybe we'll get lucky."

It would be better to explore that creepy old mansion with someone else, Cassia thought as she chewed her lip. Last night, she'd holed herself away in the back bedroom with some downloaded movies after Sarah left for the day. She could have gone exploring, but her attempt during the day to find only locked doors had not been encouraging.

Plus, every time Sarah saw Cassia walking about the mansion, she'd come smiling and asking if there was anything Cassia needed and generally hovering over Cassia. It was impossible to do anything without Sarah being right at her elbow, acting helpful, if not actually helping. If Cassia hadn't been so cowed by the trauma of finding the body and then being invaded by what seemed like the entire sheriff's department for the county and every specialist they could think of for all day Sunday, she might have set some boundaries with Sarah.

Maybe.

Cassia straightened. If she was going to stay out of jail, she would have to deal with Sarah, but that could wait until tomorrow. "Yes, come by tonight. I'll see what I can do with getting more keys. Maybe Sarah will slip up and leave them lying around and I'll steal them back." She said it as a joke, but meant every word of it.

———

Cassia cradled the wrapped package of Trent's special casserole—parting gift from the diner, as Genevieve had called it—as she walked down Main Street to where her van stood parked next to a meter. The rest of the street was empty, with the rest of the residents apparently still at the apple festival.

Genevieve had to run home and feed her cats and said she'd be over in a bit. They'd come up with a battle plan for Cassia to go home and try to get more information from Sarah before the housekeeper left for the day.

The sun hung low close to the horizon, shining brightly in Cassia's eyes as she juggled the wrapped food package onto one hip and dug around in her pants pocket for her car keys. Nearly blinded by the glare, she turned around the back of the van and almost ran into Sheriff Andrews. He had a ticket pad out and stood staring at the meter by the side of her van. He looked disappointed when he saw Cassia.

Cassia walked over to the meter. Two minutes were left. "You're kidding, right?" she asked.

His brows furrowed.

"We take rules very seriously around here," Sheriff Andrews said. "I'm starting to think you don't at all, and that's going to be a problem."

Cassia narrowed her eyes at the sheriff. Putting her keys on top of the food bag, she dug around in her pocket once again. She pulled out a quarter and held it up for Sheriff Andrews to see.

The meter made a clicking noise. They both turned to look at it. A mechanical red flag had popped up, and the time now said one minute.

Cassia walked over to the meter and slid the quarter in. The machinery chewed on the offering and sucked back the red flag and then reset the time to thirty minutes. She turned to Sheriff Andrews and gave him a sunny smile. "Rules followed."

He snapped the ticket pad shut and made a noise that sounded like a growl. Cassia stepped back.

"I hope you're taking seriously my instructions to stay in town," he said as he slipped the pad into his back pocket.

"Absolutely," Cassia said. "I only have to run this van back tomorrow."

"Run it back where? This isn't your vehicle?"

"No, it's a rental," Cassia said, pointing to the sticker on the back that said *Not Your Ratchet Rentals*. "I believe if I don't return it, they'll think I was stealing it, and that wouldn't be very rule-following of me, now would it?"

"Don't get smart with me," Sheriff Andrews said, leaning in to warn her. A familiar scent washed over Cassia, but she couldn't quite place it. It was definitely coming from Sheriff Andrews. She glanced down at the tight leather jacket he wore, clinging so closely to his biceps and shoulders that she could've traced where one muscle ended and another started.

Cassia stepped back. Sheriff Andrews followed. Cassia retreated again, this time angling the meter between the two of them to get some space.

"So, any word on who that person was at the mansion?" Cassia asked. "I thought for sure you would come back right away yesterday and tell me all about it."

"Why would I do that? That is official law enforcement information," Sheriff Andrews said.

"I don't know, because it happened at my place…"

"Because you might be a suspect. Is that what you mean?" Sheriff Andrews asked.

"I didn't do anything," Cassia said. She hated how her voice was edging on a whine. Nate had told her not to say anything, but there was something about this guy that just got under her skin.

"We'll see about that. The law makes those final decisions," Sheriff Andrews said, lifting his chin and looking down at her.

"I thought the evidence did," Cassia said.

"Like I said, we'll see. I'm not at liberty to share any information about the case at this time," Sheriff Andrews said. He turned on his heel and walked down the street. As he reached the corner, he turned and yelled back to her, "Don't go anywhere," before heading to his waiting squad car parked around the corner.

"I have a lawyer!" Cassia yelled inanely after him, then watched him go.

Why couldn't she have some of that courage when she was dealing with Sarah? Sarah was half her size. Maybe it was because Sarah didn't make her quite as angry as Mr-too-tight-clothes Sheriff Andrews did.

CHAPTER 10

Cassia drove the van through the winding road in front of the mansion. She'd already broken most of the branches trying to reach across the road on her first several passages on the drive to the mansion, and now the white rental van fit easily between the thick overgrowth and untrimmed trees lining the bumpy road. Getting through the worst of it, she made the last turn just as the sun set behind the mansion. A beautiful red glow suffused the back of the mansion and the trees behind it. It almost looked beautiful. Magical. Not like the scary dump that it normally looked like on the outside during the daytime.

Glancing at her phone in the van's console, Cassia checked the time. If Sarah kept the same schedule as she did yesterday, she should still be at the mansion. Cassia hadn't seen a vehicle out front yesterday when she had been attempting to explore the place, but Sarah had gotten there somehow. It was too far from town for someone to easily drop Sarah off and then leave again, so there must be a car parked somewhere around the mansion. Where was Sarah keeping it?

Rather than slog around by foot in the rapidly dimming twilight, Cassia turned on the headlights for the van and kept driving around the side of the mansion instead of parking out front like she normally did. The ground sloped and rolled like a badly maintained rollercoaster, but there were faint depressions in the scrubby weeds that looked like tires had flattened them. She followed them.

The tire tracks led around the west side of the mansion. After going past the front parlor, and then through what looked like an old-fashioned archway for a horse and carriage, it snaked back around to an ill kept broad gravel path with patches of weeds here and there. The remains of a partially collapsed shed, painted to match the same dull color as the house, sat at the far side of the gravel path, but looked empty from the gaping hole in its side.

The gravel pad stopped just short of the observatory tacked on the back of the mansion. It was impossible to drive behind the building any further in the van. If she wanted to go all the way around the place, she'd have to do it on foot. Maybe tomorrow. That was not something she was going to do tonight.

The reasonable place for a garage was right by the mansion, yet there was nothing.

Cassia hit the steering wheel with frustration. Taking the van on a wide swing to turn it around again, the headlights picked up a glint in the thicket of trees just past the mansion. She hit the brakes. The van skidded gracelessly to a stop on the gravel, lighting up a faint road going away from the mansion into the trees.

She glanced back at the house. Only a few windows faced this way. Shades and curtains blocked the windows on the upper stories and the window on the first floor stood empty. The first floor window probably opened to a utility room or something related to the archway for the horse and carriage and not a living space.

Chances were, Sarah wasn't watching her.

Even if she was, Cassia tried to tell herself, she wasn't doing anything wrong. This was supposed to be her property. Still, the goosebumps that rose on her scalp and neck were not convinced. Cassia rubbed her hat around on her head and then pulled it down, trying to banish the feeling of dread in her stomach.

Leaning forward, Cassia pushed the gas pedal to nudge the van forward, but hit it a little too hard and the van jolted and careened toward the nearest tree. She clutched the steering wheel tighter to guide the vehicle through the tight trees while simultaneously slowing down as quickly as she could without skidding the tires.

Luckily, the road was only narrow for a short bit, and then opened up again into another clearing inside the trees that was not easily visible from the mansion. A wide garage with four large vehicle doors faced into the clearing. Silver corrugated metal covered the front, and sides. A red steel roof covered it. It looked more like a huge utility building rather than a fancy mansion garage.

Cassia parked the van and got out. She considered leaving the door open and the vehicle running, in case she needed to make a fast getaway, but decided the greater danger was probably a raccoon crawling into the van and then attacking her when she tried to drive away. She shut the door and put the keys in her pocket.

A row of long windows ran along the short side of the garage, along with a person-sized door. Standing on tiptoe, she grabbed the ledge of the window and pulled herself up to look. The ghostly shape of a white car showed closest to the window. It looked like there were several more vehicles beyond it, but they were dark in color and there was little light inside the garage. Cassia walked to the garage door and grabbed the handle. It wouldn't turn. Locked.

Why was everything in this place always locked?

Going back to the window, Cassia tried to take another look, choosing a different side of the window to look in. It was useless. Stepping back, she rested her feet for a moment from trying to stand on tiptoe. After some consideration, Cassia ran back to the van and unlocked the door and grabbed her cell from the console. Going back to the window, she turned on the flashlight function on her phone and pressed it up to the glass to throw light inside the garage.

Four vehicles total. A large white sedan parked closest, then a low sports car, another sedan, and what looked like the top of a Model T Ford beyond it. "No way," Cassia said to herself.

"Finding anything interesting?" a chilly voice said behind Cassia.

Sarah stood behind her, one hand on her orange twill skirted hip. As always, she had a matching jacket and hat. Today she'd even outdone herself with a matching orange twill bag. An actual scowl replaced Sarah's normally perky smile. Cassia never thought she'd miss that smile.

"Just curious," Cassia said, instantly mad at herself for feeling like she had to explain anything to Sarah. "This is my place," she said, but that just made it worse because she'd said it more like a question than a statement.

Get a grip, Cassia. This woman is tiny. There's no reason to be afraid of her.

As if sensing Cassia's thoughts, Sarah stepped closer, invading Cassia's personal space. Cassia stepped back.

What was with Forgotten Valley and talking close enough to kiss?

Cassia shook her head to rid it of that image.

Sarah smiled. Cassia narrowed her eyes at the orange menace.

"Actually," Cassia said, "I need to return my rental tomorrow, and the will said something about vehicles. You know, cars, being part of the estate. I need to get one of them. Have you magically found any keys that might, say, include car keys?"

"I'm so sorry, my dear, but I have not. What did the will specifically say about the cars, may I ask?"

So, Sarah had not seen the will. She must not have gotten anything from the old lady, or she would have at least been at a reading of it.

"Oh, I can't remember the specifics right now, except for there were multiple cars. A couple newer, a couple older," Cassia said, bluffing. The will had said 'the contents of the house.' Now Cassia regretted not having a more detailed inventory. Another thing for further investigation.

"I see," said Sarah smoothly. "It's too bad you don't have more information."

"Yes, too bad. For instance, I had no idea about your presence in the house."

"It must have slipped Mrs. Mandress's mind, for I'm quite sure she took it for granted that I would always be here. I was quite indispensable to her."

"You learned the job quickly I take it," Cassia said. She watched Sarah's face closely and was not unrewarded. A dark shadow crossed Sarah's face, making it ugly for a split second before the woman smoothed her expression and restored the insincere smile.

"Yes, quite," Sarah said.

"What happened to the previous housekeeper?" Cassia asked.

"I'm quite sure I don't know," Sarah said, shifting her stance to one hip. "Are you implying something?"

"Oh no, not at all," said Cassia. She walked back to the side of the garage next to the window and tapped on the pane. "Beautiful cars in there. You take care of them too?"

"Only the one I drive," Sarah said, pulling car keys from

her orange bag. "I'd let you look around, but I have to get going and can't leave my only key here."

"Why not? Wouldn't that key technically belong to the estate?" Cassia asked, pointing to her own chest. "Meaning me."

"I'm not sure anything actually belongs to you until the probationary period is over," said Sarah.

The two women stared at each other.

"This has been a marvelous chat, but I am expected elsewhere and must get going. Perhaps we can get some clarification on the probationary period tomorrow. In the meantime," Sarah shrugged her shoulders as if it pained her to say it, "I'll not be making any changes until I hear from a lawyer."

She turned away from Cassia as if dismissing her, then dug around in her bag and clicked on an opener inside of it. The nearest garage door lifted with a groan and ran back on its chains. Inside, a new white four-door sedan trimmed in black and shiny chrome faced outward. Its lights flared, and it chirped a welcome as Sarah walked back and grabbed the driver side door to open it. She got inside and pushed a button on the dash. The engine roared to life. She flashed Cassia another insincere smile as she grabbed the seatbelt and fastened it across her body.

The car nosed out of its parking spot, the engine purring smoothly. It had almost completely passed Cassia when she bolted and hit the rear door window with her palm. The car skidded to a stop.

Sarah looked out at her as the driver's side window slowly lowered.

"What?" Sarah asked, a tinge of anger in her voice.

"You promised keys for me today, will or no will. It's been four days. Even if I'm living here for a probationary period, I need access to the grounds and the house, or it isn't really living here, is it?" Cassia said.

Sarah's lips pressed together as she stared at Cassia. "I did promise. And I kept my promise as best I could. There is a ring of keys on the kitchen island. If there are keys missing from them, then they are not keys I ever had access to. Now if you please," said Sarah, gesturing with her head to Cassia's hand still on the rear window.

"Right," said Cassia. She pulled her hand back. A distinct print of her palm and five digits shone in the dim light on the otherwise spotless window.

"Thank you," Sarah said, returning her gaze forward and not even waiting for her window to completely roll up before tearing out across the courtyard to the exit through the trees.

A tiny light shone over the license plate on the rear of the car as it drove away. The custom plate read *MANDRS4*.

"No flipping way," said Cassia. Her fingers curled into fists.

———

Cassia sat at the kitchen island, a half-empty pint of ice cream in front of her and a spoon in hand. A used plate and fork and the remains of the bag from the diner sprawled on the counter behind her. Miss Mansfield groomed herself contentedly on the stool next to Cassia.

Cassia leaned in and stared at the ring of keys in front of her as she slowly lifted another spoon of ice cream into her mouth. Ten keys. It both seemed like too many and not enough for this enormous house. There were a few vanilla keys like you would find in any budget key place for any budget generic lock, but there were also two skeleton keys, one tiny key the size of the tip of her pinky, and two keys with wide grips shaped in the form of clover leaves.

All the keys shined a uniform shiny silver under the kitchen light. All new.

Where exactly does one go to get a copy of a skeleton key?

Is that one of the skills of a really good housekeeper? Cassia snorted and shoved the spoon into the rest of the ice cream.

She glanced at the window. Full black gave away the night outside. During the day, she always forgot about the need for curtains, and then at night felt pinned inside the house. Each black maw of a window she passed by a glaring reminder that anyone outside could see in.

Except for the second floor. When she had been in the backyard, going toward the garage, those second floor windows had curtains. Perhaps all of them did behind the locked doors.

She pulled out her phone and pressed the button to check the time. Genevieve must be running late.

Grabbing an Italian roast coffee pod, she made herself another cup. The coffee might keep her up all night, but it was warm, and she still hadn't figured out the heat in the house, though at her request, Sarah had turned up the thermostat so the house no longer dropped to fifty degrees at night. It must have been set that way after the old lady died. Cassia couldn't imagine any elderly person wanting to live in a house that cold.

Unless she had been really, really, really cheap.

Well, that could have been. She hadn't known Aunt Mildred Mandress at all.

Just as Cassia hit the button to brew the coffee, a clanging noise rang out in the kitchen. Cassia jumped and accidentally pushed the coffee maker so far water splashed out of the reserve on top.

"What the heck?"

She looked around for the source of the noise. It came from a wooden box with carved curlicues on it over the doorway to the hallway. An old-fashioned doorbell.

"If anyplace could use a ring camera, it would be this place," Cassia muttered to herself as she walked to the front door. Peering through the peephole, she once again saw

Genevieve peering back at her. The entryway light hanging low over Genevieve gave her dark shadows around her eyes and an ominous look. It didn't help that she was dressed in all black and only her exposed face shone in the light, looking like a floating head.

Cassia opened the door. "Nice outfit," she said.

Unfazed, Genevieve gave her a smile. "I thought so! Not every day you get to go exploring in a huge mansion that might be haunted and a home to criminals wide and far."

Cassia put a hand on her hip. "So both haunted, and a home for criminals. Impressive. Those criminals must have nerves of steel to not be bothered by the ghosts."

"Don't most criminals have nerves of steel?" Genevieve said, pushing past Cassia and entering the house. She carried a large backpack that couldn't entirely close around the huge flashlight sticking out of the top of it.

Cassia shut the door and pointed at the backpack. "There are lights here."

Genevieve swung the backpack around and grabbed the enormous flashlight. "This is both a light and a weapon." She demonstrated by grabbing the long handle and swinging it like a baseball bat, nearly taking out a vase on the side table nearby.

"Okay, okay," Cassia said, laughing as she steadied the vase to keep it from falling to the floor. "I really don't think we'll need that, but at least we're prepared."

"You never know. Someone did die here," Genevieve said.

Cassia stopped laughing. She waved to Genevieve to follow her back to the kitchen. This time Genevieve kept up.

"These," Cassia said, pointing to the ring of keys on the counter, "are the keys I got. I waited for you to get here before trying any doors."

"Oh, I feel special."

"You should. Or maybe I just wanted a witness for

anything I did find." They were just joking, but a shiver went over Cassia and down her back. All humor aside, she hated having to explore this place at night. Maybe they should have waited till tomorrow morning before Sarah showed up, but then again, she had to go return the van tomorrow and finally get the rest of the stuff out of it if she could find a place to put it all. That was going to take all day.

"I brought all sorts of good things," Genevieve said. She plopped her backpack onto the island. There was another large flashlight, only slightly smaller than the massive one Genevieve had demonstrated, a twist of rope, a full roll of black duct tape, a tin of hairpins, two walkie-talkies, and a bag of tiny metal bits that looked like old-fashioned jacks from a kids' toy.

"What is all this? This looks like something you would need for a robbery. Or kidnapping." She raised one eyebrow at Genevieve.

"Girl, nothing happens in this town. And I watch way too many police dramas. No way I'm giving up the chance to use some of those skills." She shadowboxed in the air.

Cassia rubbed her forehead. It was going to be a long night.

The coffeemaker dinged as the last bit of coffee dripped. Cassia went to get her cup. She took a step, then turned around and lifted it to Genevieve. "Coffee?"

"Nope. I'm good to go. Let's do this thing," Genevieve said. "Come on, come on."

Cassia blew on her coffee so she could drink it faster. Genevieve definitely did not need any more caffeine.

CHAPTER 11

They made it through the rooms on the first floor quickly even though Genevieve had insisted on opening every cupboard and cabinet in each room as they went, even looking underneath furniture, even the delicate furniture in the parlors with its spindly wooden legs that couldn't have hidden much beneath them. Without fail, Genevieve reached up under each one and patted it as if looking for an envelope taped to the bottom of the furniture. If Cassia was going to hide anything, that was the last place she would do it, so maybe Genevieve was on to something. But Cassia had drawn the line when it came to the massive two-story library packed with books where Genevieve wanted to flip through the pages of each book.

"Haven't you ever seen any of those fake books, with a section cut out and a wad of cash shoved in the middle? You could be rich right now and not even know it," Genevieve said.

"Highly unlikely," Cassia said, her hand on her hip. Besides, as much as she wanted wads of cash right now, that was something she could go looking for on a regular day even when Sarah was around. They needed to get upstairs to the locked rooms. The rooms that Sarah had magically appeared by whenever Cassia went to try their doors.

"Or a secret map?" Genevieve said, reaching out to grab one of the books on the shelf near to her.

"There must be hundreds of books here, and as much as I love that, we can check that later," Cassia said. Or never.

Genevieve frowned and slowly pushed the book back into place on the shelf. "Okay, fine. You're no fun."

"I thought you were grateful that I let you come in and explore the mansion," Cassia said in an acidic tone, teasing. "You know the Smiths would be downright jealous right now. You get to see things no townsperson has in years, if ever."

"True that," said Genevieve. She broke into a grin. "Where to now, Captain?"

Cassia held up the ring of keys she had stashed in her front pocket. It felt heavy and warm from her body heat. Each key new and shiny, like a promise of adventure and riches. "Let's see what the second story holds."

They mounted one side of the paired arching stairways in the front entrance and made it to the second floor landing. It looked different at night. The high windows over the front door were black with night, leaving the upper landing in shadows and not in the bright streaming sun of the late afternoon.

"Which way?" Genevieve asked as they looked to the left and the right. Tiny mounted wall lights cast warm glows along both hallways, but were not powerful enough to truly light up the space. The left hallway was the same row of closed doors they passed by when they'd run to the tower on Cassia's first day at the mansion.

The right hallway looked different since doors only lined the side toward the front of the house. The other side of the hallway abutted the two-story library. There were no separate rooms there since the library took all that space. At the end of the right hall a light revealed another open passageway at its end, most likely leading to a stairway upstairs to the third floor. A mirror to the hallway to their left.

"Left," Cassia said. Something about having those doors locked the first time she tried them irritated her. Time to make that right.

"Left it is," Genevieve said, giving her a salute.

They entered the left hallway. Cassia selected the first door to the right. She tried the handle. Of course, the door was locked. No keyhole marred the polished brass knob, only a deadbolt keyhole below it. Ignoring the skeleton keys and the tiny one, Cassia started with the standard looking keys and worked her way through the ring. None of the standard keys would even go into the keyhole. The strange ones with the cloverleaf handles did. Finally, one turned with a solid click inside the door. The lock was heavier than she expected and took some strength to move the bolt.

"All right," Genevieve said, rubbing her hands in anticipation.

Cassia twisted the knob and pushed the door open. Her heart raced at the massive white shapes within, but then calmed when her eyes focused on white sheeting draped over what must be furniture beneath. She fumbled for a light by the doorway and found an old-fashioned switch that required one to push in a button to turn on the lights. After a second's delay, the lights reluctantly came on overhead, and one of the bare bulbs in the art deco chandelier above exploded with a soft pop. Genevieve and Cassia both jumped.

"I guess that light hasn't been used in a while," Cassia said.

A wainscot of dark wood paneling ran the circumference of the room, topped with old-fashioned floral wallpaper. A peek under the sheeting revealed dark brown, nearly black, stained heavy wood furniture. It looked old. Unlike the rest of the mansion, this room had not been updated in a long, long time.

They pulled back some of the sheeting to get a better look, but stopped when the clouds of dust sent them into fits of coughing. The shelves of the heavy armoire at the back of the room were empty, as were the drawers of the desk. It was as if the furniture had been transported directly from a furniture warehouse and stashed here, without any sign of anyone actually living with it and using it.

"Where's all her stuff?" Genevieve asked.

Cassia shook her head. "Maybe this was a guestroom." She wiped her hands on her pants. "Didn't those sheriff people come through here? It looks completely undisturbed."

"Maybe Sarah told them she couldn't find the key," Genevieve said with a smirk.

"Ha," Cassia said. "More likely they took one look and decided no one had been in this room in three decades."

Disappointed, they left the room and checked the rest of the ones in the hallway. Amazingly enough, Cassia's keys worked for all of them, but the results were all the same. Old furniture, old rooms, all empty and dusty. It was the most depressing thing Cassia had seen in a long time.

"Let's try the other hallway on this floor," Cassia said, motioning to the other side of the top landing of the entryway stairways. Genevieve nodded.

The first door on the right when they faced the hallway opened much easier than the other doors they had just tried. A newer style key fit in the lock below the knob. The light unstained sections of wood in the door around the lock gave away that the current lock was a different shape than the original one had been, and it had been replaced recently.

Sarah twisted the knob and pushed the door open. The door opened with a strange popping sound, as if the seal of a bottle had been broken, and the wave of a wretched smell washed back over them. An unpleasant mixture of hospital disinfectant and organic rot. Cassia and Genevieve coughed, wiping their eyes that watered from the acrid odor.

"Shut that door!" Genevieve said, protesting. Cassia nodded. She held her breath and leaned into the room to grab the handle and pull the door shut again. It took some force to get the tongue to click in place so she could let go of the handle and cover her mouth for more coughs.

They waved their hands in front of their faces, trying to clear away the foul air that had come out of the room.

"You know," Cassia said, when she was near the end of her coughing fit and could breathe again, "that room might actually hold something interesting."

"Like more dead people?" Genevieve asked. She looked skeptical.

"It didn't smell that bad," said Cassia.

Actually, it might have.

Genevieve crossed her arms and stared at Cassia. "You're probably right," she said reluctantly, "but we need masks or something if we're going to go in there again."

Since neither one of them had masks, they had to settle for using some of Cassia's retro bandannas tied over their mouths. It probably didn't help at all, but psychologically it felt better to have something rather than nothing when facing the door again.

Once they were ready, Cassia in a pink bandanna and Genevieve in purple, Cassia gripped the door again and pushed it open. They stared inside, trying not to breathe.

Unlike the other rooms on the second floor, this one was furnished with light wood flooring abutting to a section of linoleum near the windows. Light yellow paint covered the walls from floor to ceiling. Instead of being filled with masses of dark furniture, only three things stood underneath sheeting. Cassia walked into the room to the one object resting squarely in the middle of the linoleum section of the floor and pulled up the sheet to take a peek underneath. A hospital bed. A full-on modern hospital bed with wheels and electronic attachments and plastic railing. "Holy cow," she said.

Genevieve peered underneath the sheeting of a waist-high object pushed up against one of the long walls, then pulled off the sheeting with a flair.

Cassia turned to object to the cloud of dust that came off, but stopped short when she saw the enormous electronic device. It was a cross between a small car and the control panels they always showed in movies of airplane cockpits. "What is that?" Cassia asked.

"Beats me," Genevieve said. "Aren't you the scientist type? I thought you'd know."

Cassia shook her head slowly. She went to the device and looked at all the knobs and dials. Two tiny display screens were set in the vertical portion near the back of the device. What were they supposed to display? Whatever it was, it was old, and must've been very expensive at the time. The display screens had the curve of old CRT screens.

The only other piece of furniture in the room was an old-fashioned metal cabinet. Cassia expected it to be full of medical supplies and bandages, but like every other piece of furniture on the second floor, its shelves stood empty.

"Where's the smell coming from?" asked Genevieve.

Cassia swung around. Her eyes fixed on the hospital bed. Her feet moved forward almost against her will and she lifted the sheet and leaned only slightly forward to sniff the mattress. She gagged and dropped the sheet again. Without a word, she turned and pointed at it to Genevieve and then left the room as quickly as she could. Genevieve followed, nearly stepping on Cassia's feet in her haste. Genevieve grabbed the door and shut it after her with a little more force than was necessary.

"Why would they not burn that thing?" Cassia said, incredulous. "Everything else is cleared out, why leave a biohazard mattress."

"Someone probably did die on that thing," Genevieve said.

Cassia had to agree.

This inheritance was starting to feel like a curse.

Untying the knot behind her head keeping the pink bandanna over her mouth, Cassia pulled it off and let it fall to the hall floor in disgust.

Maybe it was the hospital bed, and all the horrible memories of hospitals it brought back for Cassia, or maybe it was the four days of strange things happening, and Sarah's terrible attitude and never actually being helpful, but Cassia was starting to get angry. She felt the hard little knot in her belly and knew it would grow unless she did something about it. Her mind hardened in resolve.

If someone died a horrible death in that room, she was going to find out who was responsible, just as she would for that poor guy they'd found hanging from the observatory dome. No one deserved to die like that, just as no one deserved to die in some locked away room in a creepy mansion.

Now it went way beyond keeping herself out of jail and keeping the mansion.

She couldn't do anything for her parents, but she could do something about what happened here. Perhaps Aunt Mildred hadn't been in such complete control of everything as Cassia first thought.

Cassia looked down the remaining doors in the hallway and the passage to the stairwell beyond. "Right. Let's do this thing."

Genevieve eyed her, taking in Cassia's steely expression.

CHAPTER 12

Cassia sat at the kitchen island, her eyes slightly unfocused with exhaustion as Genevieve rummaged around in the enormous double fridge so deeply that only her butt showed by the open doorway from Cassia's angle. Genevieve reemerged from the fridge, triumphant, holding a package of processed meat with little flecks of green and red in it.

"Ah-ha. Whoever does the shopping here has great taste," Genevieve said. She tossed the package of meat onto the kitchen island and dove back into the fridge for bread, lettuce, mustard, and a package of coleslaw mix.

"That would be Sarah," Cassia said. She had not really looked too closely inside the fridge, having only done most of her meal shopping from the massive freezer section.

"I think I want a Sarah. And a mansion and budget to go with it."

Cassia snorted. "Oh no, you do not."

"But look at all this food," Genevieve said, pointing to the spread on the island countertop.

"Is that even food?" asked Cassia. She picked up the

package of lunch meat and examined it, turning the package over.

"That, my dear, is the food of the gods. Pimento loaf. They don't even sell it in Forgotten Valley. You have to drive at least one town over to get it, sometimes two. I haven't bothered in a while. Stupid car," Genevieve said, her voice trailing off as she got engrossed in opening the bread and grabbing a plate for herself. She looked up at Cassia with the plate still in her hand. "Sandwich?"

Cassia nodded numbly. They had gone through the entire second floor and found nothing but old furniture and lots and lots of dust. Well, nothing except that horrible room with the old rotten hospital bed. The third floor was next on the list but they had both agreed a break was in order before tackling another whole floor of possibly dirty rooms.

Gleefully, Genevieve put her sandwich together, squeezing more mustard on the lunch meat and lettuce than Cassia thought anyone could ever want on a single sandwich. She took a huge bite and chewed on it thoughtfully. She swallowed, then held up a thumb. "Perfect." She made an identical sandwich, mustard and all, and slid it across the counter to Cassia.

After eating half of the offering, grimacing a bit at the saltiness of the meat and the mustard together, Cassia started to feel better. Her exhaustion and hunger cleared away a little and she could think better.

"Thank you," she said to Genevieve. "I don't do that well when I'm hungry."

Genevieve winked at her. "I noticed." Genevieve's all-black outfit was now various shades of gray from all the dirt and dust they'd encountered. A large streak along her back showed where she had backed up into a coat rack and the sheeting covering it had fallen directly on her, depositing all of its dust on her instead of the floor. Dirt even covered her face, giving her the look of a superhero ninja. Cassia felt her own limp locks and wondered how Genevieve got hers to stick up in such a stylish way.

Considering how many people had been trampling through the house the day they found the body, Cassia was surprised there was so much dust left in the rooms. Maybe Sheriff Andrews brought it in himself just to drive Cassia nuts.

"Do you know, I think Sarah's driving one of the mansion cars," Cassia said.

Genevieve stopped chewing and stared at her. She swallowed. "How do you know?"

"The license plate said Mandress four. It didn't have all the letters, but it was clearly meant to say Mandress. There is no way she would get the license plate for her own car just because she was working here." Cassia pushed her plate away.

"Probably not," Genevieve agreed. "Maybe it was a condition of employment here, though."

"That's the thing. I didn't even know about her till I got here. There was nothing in the will about her. And she keeps talking about taking care of this place is if she owns it and I don't even know the terms of her employment." Cassia's complaints came out in a rush. They seemed so reasonable when she said them, yet Sarah could make her feel so stupid with just a glance, as if Cassia should know something she doesn't.

"That's strange," Genevieve said. She pulled the bread and lunch meat closer to make herself another sandwich. "This is your place… you should be able to fire her, right?"

"That's what I thought," Cassia said.

Genevieve quickly made a second sandwich for herself. "Are we still returning the van tomorrow?"

Cassia nodded. "I looked up the place. About fifty miles south."

Pausing in her sandwich making, Genevieve looked up and raised her eyebrows.

"I'll pay for gas," Cassia said.

Genevieve didn't move.

"And dinner," Cassia said, offering. She couldn't afford much more. She mouthed the word please. Genevieve finally nodded.

"I'm having a third sandwich," Genevieve said, laying out two more pieces of bread. "And taking a doggy bag home."

"How about a kitty bag?" said Cassia with a smirk.

Meow! came the protest from Miss Mansfield's bed on the back counter. The tiny black cat glared at Cassia, then stood and stretched.

"Not you, princess," Cassia said with a laugh. Knowing it would impress Genevieve, Cassia walked to the pantry door and opened it with a flourish, displaying row after row of canned cat food.

"Holy buckets," Genevieve said. "My cats are eating well today."

Miss Mansfield hissed from her bed on the desk. This time, Cassia turned and stared at the cat. Sometimes she swore the black feline could understand the exact words she was saying. Just in case, she addressed Miss Mansfield, "Don't worry, you can afford to share some. I'll get you more. You'll never know anything was gone."

Miss Mansfield blinked her gold eyes at Cassia, then turned in a circle and lay down with her back to Cassia.

Cassia whirled at the soft chuckle behind her. Genevieve stood with her hand over her mouth, trying not to make any noise. She finally pulled herself together and smoothed her face into a serious expression. "You know you're on the bottom of the pecking order in this entire house, don't you?" She grabbed the groceries on the counter and backed away when Cassia tried to hit her with a crumpled up napkin. "Don't kill the messenger," Genevieve protested, then shoved the food back into the fridge.

Grumbling to herself, Cassia gathered the used dishes and set them in the sink. She took a deep breath and exhaled slowly. Genevieve wasn't wrong. Maybe that's why it made her so crabby.

"Shall we go find all the secrets of this creepy estate?" Genevieve asked, smiling to cajole Cassia.

Cassia nodded.

———

They decided to resume with the third floor by going up the stairwell at the end of the hallway on the right side of the landing, the side that had the horrible hospital bed. The stairway at the far end of the hall was much wider than the stairway they had gone up to access the tower. This seemed much more like an area meant for a lot of traffic. It was wide enough for large furniture to be brought up, and servants to walk up and down, passing each other with trays and other things, as Cassia imagined they had at one point in the past for this ancient mansion. It was definitely a place that had to have servants to run well. No housewife or househusband could caretake such a large place by themselves.

They mounted the stairway and took the steps up and through two one hundred and eighty degree turns, and then yet another hundred and eighty degree turn to reach the top. It seemed like too many steps to go up one floor, but Cassia was distracted from that thought when they reached the top. Instead of opening into a hallway with doors off of it, it opened into a large space that bloomed out much like the entryway to the front door two flights below them. At the back of the space, two large double doors stood shut.

The space was large enough for a small cocktail party.

Beyond it, the third floor looked to be one gigantic room hidden beyond the double doors.

"Whoa," Genevieve said. Cassia silently agreed.

Unlike the modern remodel of the first floor, or the dark wood and old style of the second floor, this entryway embraced all the excesses of the baroque period. Curved and intricate cream colored molding covered light blue walls, creating a complete yet pleasing pattern. Even more intricate molding surrounded the doors themselves, climaxing at a peak of flourishes above the double doors. The doors themselves were the only unpainted wood in the entire room, instead covered in a thick layer of lacquer and shining with the depth of amber.

The size of the space was deceptive. It looked normal until Cassia strode forward and reached the doors to try the handles. Rather than normal sized doors, these reached up to over twice her height, and equally wide. She felt tiny.

Of course, the doors were locked. She pulled on one of them, but it was so heavy it barely budged against the bolt. Twisting dragons inscribed the large ornate lock plate beneath the handle, inset with two key holes.

Two key holes? How does that work?

Genevieve stared over her shoulder as Cassia touched the holes gently. The edges were worn smooth. The locks must be antiques themselves.

The only keys that fit were the two skeleton keys. Cassia tried to unlock the door using one, then the other, then in frustration, put both keys in at the same time and tried to twist them in various combinations. She tried so many things at once that when the lock finally clicked, she wasn't even sure what motions had done it.

Backing up, she pocketed the keys and took in a deep breath.

Over her shoulder, Genevieve raised her flashlight, ready to strike in case anything came running out the doors when opened. Cassia almost told her to stop, but hesitated. Perhaps it wasn't such a bad idea.

Gripping the handles, Cassia pulled both doors open at once. They gave with a creak.

Cassia and Genevieve stared into the enormous room.

CHAPTER 13

They stood in the entryway, listening, and letting their eyes adjust to the dim light let in by the few windows with their curtains cracked open. Nothing moved within the vast space. Belatedly, Cassia realized they were standing with the light behind them and would have been an easy target if anything had been within. Her face heated as she nudged Genevieve, then quickly moved inside the room and out of the doorway with the excuse of looking for a light switch on the wall. Nothing on her side.

Genevieve had better luck searching the other wall. A click sounded, and then again a delay as light bulbs turned on inside the many crystal chandeliers hanging in the space above, sending facets of light everywhere, along with the soft yellow glow of the bulbs.

Even the bulbs were ancient. They were no modern style Cassia recognized.

Cassia had once gone on a tour of the Schönbrunn Palace in Vienna, Austria. One of her classmates worked for the airlines at night, schlepping passenger bags from the airplane to the baggage carousel, all for the benefit of cheap tickets for the summer. Her classmate had gotten sick of going on trips by herself and offered Cassia a free ride if she'd go to Vienna with her. In a rare impulsive moment, sick of her classwork, and wanting to know what it was like to live with money, Cassia had agreed. It seemed like a bargain. All she had to do was go with the full-on tourist itinerary devised by her classmate. That included a tour of the famous palace, of course.

The scale of the rooms alone in Schönbrunn Palace had hurt her brain. These were private apartments of human beings that could have held an entire school in each one. The ornateness of the furnishings within the palace had been relentless, each item desperately trying to outdo the next with scrollwork and inlaid gold and master craftsmanship. The whole scene had soon stunned her brain into numbness.

This room could have been the architect's next project after Schönbrunn.

The walls had the same decorative ornate molding as the entryway outside, but even fancier, something Cassia would not have thought possible if asked five minutes ago. Patterns of carved and painted wood covered the light green paint of the walls below them.

A large platform on the far side of the room held a bed that looked to be twenty feet by twenty feet, along with four posters and a full canopy of curtains along the sides and top. The Maltese pattern of its covering cleverly hid the seams needed to make a covering that large.

Around the room, groupings of furniture formed little sitting areas and workspaces. Cassia counted at least three desks, and two other pieces of furniture that could have been desks with their tops folded up. The windows, which looked normal on the outside, were anything but on the inside: floor to ceiling curtains three layers deep of nested materials Cassia could tell were thick and expensive even from a distance graced each window.

Cassia's mouth felt dry.

She turned at Genevieve's heavy breathing. Genevieve stared into the room, her eyes shining strangely.

"They didn't talk about this much in town, huh?" asked Cassia, trying to be nonchalant.

Genevieve slowly shook her head, transfixed by the spectacle, for once speechless.

While they stood there, Miss Mansfield daintily entered the room, walking as if it was the most familiar place in the world to her. That helped snap Cassia out of it. They had limited time, and needed to search this place for any clues of why someone might have died here the other day, and why someone might want Cassia out of the mansion.

"Okay," Cassia said, clapping her hands, "let's get to it."

Genevieve's eyes slid to hers and slowly focused. The purpose returned to her face, and she gave Cassia a salute. "Yes, Captain."

They searched the room carefully, starting with the bed on the platform. It was easier than the other rooms because the furniture stood uncovered. The room looked ready for use today, as if just waiting for them.

Except it was stone-cold empty of anything interesting.

There was nothing under the bed. Nor in the bureaus, nor in the desk drawers, not even in the tiny drawers in the end tables. The shelves, where unfaded spots on the painted wood gave way that things had once rested there, stood empty.

The beautiful space had not a single scrap of a personal item in it. It was worse than a museum piece that would have at least had photos and other items to place the museum goers in the time of the people that lived there. Cassia's heart began to hurt, and the pain increased with each empty drawer. How could someone's life be erased so completely? The will had only listed her as the sole beneficiary. Everything should still be here, unless Aunt Mildred had spent her last days throwing away all of her personal possessions, only to keel over dead when the task was complete.

Hardly likely.

Now, it was as if Aunt Mildred Mandress was a legend and not a real human being. Human beings left scraps of paper, letters, knickknacks, things they got attached to. Cassia had yet to find a single such item in this house.

Morosely, Cassia shoved in the bottom drawer of the bureau she'd been examining.

"Hey," Genevieve called, waving Cassia over to where she was standing in front of a closed secretary desk, "this one's locked." Genevieve pulled on the wood slab of the desk and rattled the lock.

Hope stuttered alive in Cassia's chest. She ran over, pulling out the key ring from her pocket as she went. Grabbing the one tiny key, she slipped it into the keyhole at the top of the desk and twisted. The lock snapped open with a satisfying thud. Genevieve eagerly pulled down the desk lid.

Empty.

They both worked at the tiny drawers inside the top of the desk, Cassia to the left and Genevieve to the right, pulling them open and feeling toward the back. Every single one held exactly nothing.

Disgusted, Cassia stood and put her hands on her hips. Genevieve continued to search through the desk, pushing at the wood all over as if she was kneading dough.

"What are you doing?" Cassia asked.

"Checking for secret compartments," said Genevieve. At Cassia's huff, she stopped and glared at Cassia. "Are you telling me you've never watched a single mystery show ever? There are always secret compartments. Always. There's probably a message from your aunt in there for you that she was hiding from the bad guys."

Cassia raised both eyebrows.

"Oh for… have you been raised under a rock? Who doesn't know this stuff?"

Me, apparently, Cassia thought. While she hadn't grown up under a large piece of granite, she had spent a lot more time in the library studying than watching any TV shows. Not that she could even afford a television with her lowly part-time job wages, and tuition and books had completely eaten the scholarship money. Who knew she'd come to find out that made her unfit to live in normal society.

"Have you checked under all the chairs yet? You already taught me today it's another thing we should be doing," Cassia said, sarcastically.

"Not yet," Genevieve said, completely serious as she resumed massaging the desk.

Cassia shook her head and walked to the platform the bed stood on. Dropping down, she sat on the floor with her back to the bed and observed the room and Genevieve. It must be three o'clock in the morning, and suddenly she could feel it in her bones. The whole night searching had yielded nothing but a pile of old furniture. While that was good enough for selling if she needed money, it gave her no information that was going to keep her out of jail, or any clue about the guy who came to such an ignominious end a few days ago outside.

She let her head fall back on the bed large enough to be a small lake.

Miss Mansfield jumped from chair to chair, then down to the soft plush carpeting, the same rose color as the hallway and stairs outside, and ran from one side of the room to the next. She stopped with her paws splayed and ears back; her back higher than her front. After a second, she ran again, and whirled to stop with her back arched. Cassia rolled her head to one side to watch the display of the full-on zoomies.

After running across the room again, Miss Mansfield skidded

to a stop again, this time flipping on her back and grabbing something with her paws underneath one of the armchairs in the furniture arrangement just across the room from where Cassia sat. The cat continually batted whatever it was under the chair and the object flapped, sending shadows flickering on the wall behind her.

Genevieve stood up, looking around to see the source of the noise. Cassia pointed to the cat and the chair.

"She's going to destroy that," Cassia said. "Maybe that's why the room was locked."

Genevieve walked over to the chair, bent down to look under it , then grabbed something from underneath it. Triumphant, she stood up holding an envelope high. "I told you."

"You're kidding," said Cassia.

"Does this look like kidding?" Genevieve said, waving the envelope. She examined the outside of it. "Right on two counts." Walking over to Cassia, she dropped the envelope in Cassia's lap.

The outside of the envelope only had two initials, C. L.

"To you," Genevieve said. "You already owe me dinner, so I bet you a breakfast it's from your aunt."

Stunned, Cassia held the envelope and watched as Genevieve checked every single other chair and sofa and even underneath the armoires and desks. At last, after checking under the console by the big double doors, Genevieve looked back to Cassia and shook her head. She walked back and joined Cassia sitting on the platform.

"Aren't you going to open it?" Genevieve asked.

Cassia held the envelope in her shaking hands. It finally hit her why. Her parents had been gone for years now. And her grandparents before them. She thought her time of having a family was long over. Now, in her hands she held something from someone she was related to, and it was addressed directly to her. Or at least her initials, which meant if it wasn't for her, then it was a cruel trick of the universe.

"Come on," Genevieve said, coaxing Cassia. "It can't be any worse than what's already happened in your short week at this place."

Good point.

Cassia slipped a finger under the thick flap and gently pried open the envelope. It was lined with silver foil. Cripes, this envelope might have even cost more than half of her clothing. Inside was only a stiff piece of paper the size of a business card with a series of numbers on it. The top line was a phone number with a 212 area code, but the bottom line was a strange series of three sets of numbers separated by commas. They looked familiar to Cassia, but she couldn't quite place how: 299, 792, 458.

"Is that some sort of code or something?" asked Genevieve.

Cassia shrugged her shoulders. Disappointment hung heavy in her chest. She wasn't sure what she expected, maybe a heartfelt letter, or a long tale of some family secret, but getting nineteen numbers on a piece of paper was about the least satisfying thing she could have thought of.

Yes, she was good at numbers, but this was a cruel legacy even by her own standards.

CHAPTER 14

"Come on, come on, come on…," Cassia muttered to the big truck as it vibrated down Highway 71. Not being flush with a lot of extra cash, she had tried to judge just how little she could leave in the tank before returning the truck. She might have misjudged by a mile or ten. "Come on, truck, just make it to the next exit and I promise I will buy you some more fuel." See? This is what she got for being too cheap. Ted would have laughed his ass off. He loved calling her cheap.

It wasn't entirely her fault, though. Her brain was half addled from only getting a few hours asleep. Genevieve had left around five a.m., after making herself another set of sandwiches, packing some cat food, and generally driving Cassia nuts trying to figure out what the numbers on the piece of paper meant.

They'd been so preoccupied with the puzzle on the note card that Cassia had entirely forgotten to ask Genevieve to help her unload the truck. Luckily, Cassia had left her ugly paisley sofa back in California, as well as her cheap bed and frame, so she was able to unload all the boxes herself this morning. Why she had waited an entire week to unload her stuff, Cassia couldn't understand.

Actually, she could. It was terrible work, and she didn't like doing terrible work. Plus, with all the drama going on she'd sort of forgotten.

The weather had warmed up enough with the emergence of the sun that it almost felt like a summer day. Warm air blew over the top of the partially open window of the truck, bringing the scent of pine trees and mint. Cassia smiled to herself. She'd not realized how happy good weather made her.

As if sensing her mood, the truck stopped vibrating so intensely and calmed into a smoother ride. They topped over one gentle sloping hill. The tall sign of a truck stop gas station shown green and red in the distance.

"All right, we're almost there, you can do it," Cassia said, patting the dashboard of the truck.

They rolled in to a spot next to a pump just as the truck gave a final sputter and died all on its own. Cassia glanced down at the fuel gauge. A quarter past empty. "Wow. Good job, Truckster," she said, patting the dash once again. A woman in a red coat and with an even redder dye job turned to stare at Cassia. Cassia flushed, waved at the woman awkwardly, and rolled up her window. Whatever. She was one hundred percent confident that her encouragement got them to the gas station and not stalled on the side of the road two miles back.

Cassia got her gas, carefully putting in two full gallons this time, then moved the truck from its spot blocking the pump to the rear of the gas station—the only place she found a spot large enough to park the twelve-foot beast. If she was going to stop to take care of the truck, then she was going to get coffee for herself too, and that was all there was to it.

Walking around the side of the gas station, she went in. She loved truck stops. Row after row of snacks and goodies, a coffee selection so large you could find just about any machine you wanted— with café au lait, hot chocolate, fancy creamers, and stuff you didn't even know existed. All for less than a few bucks each. It was a poor student's dream.

It must have been a quiet time for truckers because only she and the cashier, a bored looking girl staring at her phone, were in the station. A few trucks were parked outside, but their drivers were nowhere to be seen. Perhaps in the showers, Cassia thought, or hanging out in the cabs of their own vehicles.

Perfect. She could take her time shopping without being in anyone's way.

Cassia grabbed the largest coffee cup she could find and tapped the edge on her bottom lip as she stared at the selections. Definitely a good base of brew coffee, but then what to put on top? Café mocha? Hazelnut?

The bells over the entrance rang.

Cassia glanced over the rack of camouflage jackets between her and the entrance and only saw the top of some red hair. She went back to her serious selection of coffee. Always her favorite beverage of the day, it was even more important when she'd only had a bit of sleep. The urn labeled Columbia roast was the fullest, which meant it probably was the most recently brewed, so Cassia pulled the lever of that pot and filled her cup halfway. Heels clicked on the linoleum behind her and then continued down another aisle.

She was just about to grab the mocha lever when an angry voice hissed, "What are you doing here?"

Cassia jumped. No one stood behind her.

"I told you I never wanted to see you again," the voice continued. A woman's voice.

A familiar voice.

"Are you going to the mansion today?" a male voice asked. Not a familiar one.

Mansion?

"That is none of your business," the familiar voice said.

"Half of everything you have is my business. More. You owe everything to me," the male voice said, so low and angry as to be almost a growl.

Whoa, thought Cassia. Not someone I want to meet in a dark alley.

Or in a dark observatory. The second thought came unbidden to her mind. A chill overcame Cassia, and she felt suddenly light-headed. She grabbed the counter and slid her cup onto it.

"Leave me alone, and stop following me," the familiar female voice said. "I'll file a complaint."

"Try me," he said back. "Nothing wrong with using a public restroom."

"Don't pull that on me," she said.

"You came in here after me. Explain that," he said, countering, full of smug satisfaction.

Silence. Apparently, the woman couldn't.

Hesitating between dread and curiosity, Cassia pushed away from the counter and walked as quietly as she could in the direction of the voices. Between the racks of chips and pretzels, she could see two people one aisle over. Pretending to look at a package of ruffled potato chips, Cassia leaned in to hear more.

"Just leave me alone. It's a regular job, that's it. For the last time, stop bothering me," the woman said.

Over the potato chips, Cassia caught a glimpse of Sarah Rheton backing up from a large man dressed in a serious imitation of a lumberjack in a red and black check jacket and matching hat. He towered over Sarah, who today was wearing a light violet ensemble. It was not the red haired woman from outside, as Cassia had thought at first. It was the red haired woman who worked at the mansion and apparently had man problems.

"I'll stop bothering you when our deal is done," he said. "And I'm the one who judges when it's done."

Sarah stared up at her less than friendly friend. She looked determined, more than afraid, something that impressed Cassia. Considering how tiny Sarah was, it actually was really impressive she was not cowering from that mountain of a man.

Frustrated, the man slammed the rack of nuts by Sarah's head before stalking off and shoving both doors wide open in his dramatic exit. Cassia jumped back, startled at the sudden rocking of the display shelving between the two rows, and fell back into the other side of the chip aisle, sending several bags skittering on the floor. She swiftly scrambled to pick them up, keeping her face low and hidden beneath her hair as Sarah walked by to grab a soda out of the fridge and then went by again to go to the counter.

Peeking occasionally through her fingers, Cassia kept her face turned away until Sarah paid and exited out the door. Once her housekeeper was gone, Cassia exhaled in relief and slid to the floor.

What the heck was going on? Was that huge thing parading as a man going to come to the mansion? What deal could he and Sarah possibly have? More questions and possible scenarios than Cassia could even list flowed through her head, and too many of them ended with Cassia running for her life on the rose colored carpet of the mansion.

"You okay back there?" the cashier called.

Cassia looked up questioningly. "Yeah, fine. Um, how…"

"Mirror," called the cashier. Cassia looked up and saw the curved mirror in the corner of the ceiling, revealing the rows of merchandise below, and Cassia herself on the floor.

"Oh, good thing. Just slipped. I'll be fine in a moment," Cassia called. She stood and dusted herself off.

Forget half coffee, half sweet. She was going full-on mocha today.

Cassia pulled up to the rental place just as her phone died. In her bleary exhaustion, she'd forgotten her charger. Luckily, Genevieve would be driving back and she should know the way. Or at least have a working phone.

The rental place was at the end of a long nondescript strip mall, a few blocks off Highway 71. Everything was various shades of gray and white and a dirty black. Even the beautiful sunny day and green grass growing nearby couldn't cheer up this place. It had none of the touristy goodness of Forgotten Valley, instead relying on the steady business of the nearby highway. Well, she wouldn't have to stay long.

Cassia parked the truck in front of the returns address. The building wasn't marked with any business name, only the address in tacky gold letters stuck to the glass door. She double-checked the paperwork in the glove box. Yep, this was it.

It was short work to open the back of the truck and double-check that she had gotten everything out and clean out the garbage and chuck it in a nearby bin. She tried to ignore the knot in her stomach at the thought of getting rid of the only vehicle she had at the moment. Her bike worked fine on campus, but it was quite the ride out from the mansion into town, and winter hadn't even started yet.

Oh well. One problem at a time. There were four cars in that garage at the mansion, and she was guessing at least one, if not all of them, were technically hers, if she could wrestle them away from Sarah. And whoever else might be trying to take the mansion. A shiver that not even the bright sunshine could keep away passed over her.

By the time she came back out of the depressing single room facility, receipt in hand, Genevieve's blue 1986 Honda Accord was waiting outside in the parking lot. Genevieve waved out the open window at Cassia.

"You made it," Cassia called, walking over to the vehicle. Genevieve leaned over and popped open the passenger side door. Cassia got in, and out of habit patted her pockets to make sure she had her wallet and her phone. As always, Genevieve's hair was a perfect spiky stylish rendition. This time, she wore a maroon outfit with a strange set of straps all over it. It looked really trendy. Of course, Cassia had no idea what the trend was or where it came from, but at least she knew she was ignorant of it.

Groceries filled the backseat of the Honda, with cases of drinks on the floor, and brown bags filling the backseat. Even more groceries sat on the back ledge, shoved into every corner and partially blocking the driver's view.

Attaching her seatbelt, Cassia pointed at the groceries in the backseat. "Hungry much?"

"Hey, if I'm gonna burn the gas to come all the way down here, I'm gonna stock up at the big store," Genevieve said, smirking at Cassia.

"I'm paying for the gas," Cassia said, as if that made a difference.

"Good thing, too," Genevieve said. She turned the key, and the engine turned over, remarkably smooth for such an old car.

Cassia twisted around in her seat to look at all the bags. She wasn't much of a grocery shopper herself, tending to forget to eat until she was really hungry and then eating a lot of whatever was close. At the university the grocery store had been a block away, which meant she didn't really have to plan ahead. If she didn't want to starve out at the mansion that might have to change. Still, that was an impressive amount of food for one person.

"More in the trunk?" Cassia asked.

"Nah, the trunk's rusted shut. I spend my car maintenance money on the engine, which is good for you," said Genevieve, giving Cassia a wink before pulling out of the parking lot. "Besides, some of that stuff is bribe food."

Irrationally Cassia hoped that meant some of the food was for her. "Oh really? How so?"

"Roger the maintenance guy seems to do better work when you have some of his favorite foods around. Cash doesn't seem to hold the same appeal, something I just don't understand," Genevieve said. "His taste in food is a little, um, shall we say hard-to-find?"

Cassia had to laugh. "It can't be more strange than pimento loaf."

Genevieve shot her a dirty look out of the corner of her eye. "So, you're considering walking home…"

"No! I kid. I kid. It's delicious, food of the gods," Cassia said, backpedaling, still unable to stop laughing. "Okay, I bite. What is it that he likes that's so hard to find?"

"Fish and malt balls. And by fish, I mean all kinds of fish. The kind that comes out of the lake, that's no problem in northern Minnesota, it's the candy Swedish fish and the other strange fish that is harder to come by—pickled herring in jars, tins of sardines. I swear, it's the weirdest thing. So I got some fancy fish and candies just for Roger in those bags." Genevieve motioned to the backseat with a thumb.

"You have that much work for a handyman? Where do you live, in a run-down shack?" Cassia slapped a hand over her mouth after the words came out. Idiot, idiot, idiot. Everyone probably lived in a shack compared to that freaking mansion she was in. Luckily, Genevieve seemed to take no offense and just chuckled.

"Not for me, silly. For the diner. We keep a stock there to make sure Roger comes quickly if we need some help. Nothing worse than having to close the dining room because of an electrical issue."

They rode in silence for a few minutes. There was little

traffic on the road, and the passing pine trees created a mesmerizing rhythm.

"Actually, I have another reason for getting so much stuff for Roger," Genevieve said, a mischievous look on her face.

Cassia turned her face away from the window to stare lazily at Genevieve. "Oh?"

"He does all the maintenance work for the sheriff's office, too."

"So?"

"The sheriff won't tell you anything about the person we found at your house. The one who keeps hinting that you might be charged," Genevieve said, circling her hand, motioning for Cassia to think about it.

Oh, that sheriff.

"I'm still confused," Cassia said. "How does that help me?"

"You never know. It's just the oddest thing how sometimes Roger can just slip and trip and his phone takes a picture of some paperwork that might have some important information on it." Genevieve said. "You know, accidentally."

"No..." Cassia sat up.

Genevieve nodded seriously. "Never underestimate the power of a malt ball."

CHAPTER 15

Cassia lay on her bed on the first floor bedroom that she had selected on her first night in the mansion. Packed boxes from California filled the room, making it feel much smaller. Her phone sat charging on one of the stacks of boxes, the charging cable looping lazily down around the cardboard and disappearing behind the box to the wall behind.

The late afternoon sun did not reach her room, making it feel even darker than it was outside. Without the van, the mansion felt even more like a prison.

Cassia rolled her head to look at the nightstand of the bed. She'd unpacked her astrophysics books and stacked them there next to the stainless steel and white linen lamp. There was no pressing need for them right now, but having them out was a familiar comfort. She reached out and grabbed the toy telescope she'd set up next to them. It, too, was banished to the middle of nowhere until she could get it together for a different program next year. Cassia set the telescope on her stomach, placed both hands behind her head, and stared at the ceiling.

Sarah was somewhere around the mansion. Cassia knew she had to confront her and get the keys to one of the cars but wasn't feeling up to it, not today. Besides, she would feel more prepared with some information from the lawyer after her upcoming second meeting. Hopefully, he'd had success getting some information from the law firm named in the will, or at least understood it better than she did.

Of course, that might be a lot to ask because he was also supposed to keep her out of jail for a murder she didn't commit, if it even was a murder.

Cassia closed her eyes. One thing at a time. She had to get through tonight and tomorrow. As long as it didn't rain tomorrow, biking into town for her meeting with the lawyer would be fine. She'd deal with the car stuff afterwards.

Cassia's stomach growled. After Genevieve had called for a rain check on dinner and then dropped her off, Cassia had run to the kitchen, fed Miss Mansfield, then microwaved the family size pad Thai she found in the back of the freezer and took it with a fork back to her room. Either Cassia ate more food than the average family, or they were lying on the package, because Cassia wanted a second serving of dinner. Listening to her stomach complain, she weighed the risks of running into Sarah if she ventured to the kitchen again.

Her stomach let out one especially loud grumble. Cassia opened her eyes, startled at her own body. Miss Mansfield eyed her from her spot at the foot of the bed and put one paw on Cassia's leg.

"What do you think? Should I go get more food?" Cassia asked the feline.

Miss Mansfield blinked slowly at her.

"I think I need a codebook to understand you," Cassia said.

Cassia pushed the telescope to the side and then pressed a hand on her stomach to stop its rumbling. That worked. That decided it, no more food for now.

Besides, if Sarah was here, perhaps that scary looking

lumberjack guy was snooping around too. Genevieve had no idea who the guy could have been when Cassia described the man she'd seen with Sarah.

"Flannel and hat," Genevieve had said, "you've just described nearly every man in northern Minnesota."

"But he was big," Cassia said, protesting.

All that got from Genevieve was one raised eyebrow. Apparently a lot of men were big in northern Minnesota. Must have something to do with the air up here.

Genevieve had offered to let Cassia stay with her that night. Cassia seriously considered it, but then remembered Miss Mansfield. Someone must have taken care of the feline before Cassia got there, probably Sarah, but she didn't have Sarah's phone number to call and ask her to feed Miss Mansfield before leaving. She did take Sheriff Andrews' direct number from Genevieve. "How do you have this?" Cassia asked. "You know, the diner," Genevieve said, waving off the question but not meeting Cassia's eyes.

A knock at the bedroom door startled Cassia. She sat up, disturbing the plate on the bed next to her, and barely catching it before it slid to the floor.

"Hello?" Cassia asked.

"Miss Lemon, I'm leaving for the day. Is there anything else you need?" Sarah said through the door.

Anything else? Car keys would be nice.

Cassia rose from the bed and opened the door, pushing some boxes out of the way to try to open it further. She'd made rather a mess looking for her pajamas, which she still couldn't find.

Sarah stood in the doorway, surveying the room with her nose wrinkled. She wore the same pale violet outfit Cassia had seen earlier in the day. That had definitely been her at the gas station.

"Haven't unpacked yet," Cassia said, then silently berated

herself for feeling the need to make an excuse to someone who was supposed to be her employee.

"I see."

"Have you found anything about the cars yet? I mean, I would like a set of car keys, please." Cassia tried to turn the question into a direct command but didn't quite manage it, her voice trailing up and sounding unsure at the end.

"I'm working on it," Sarah said, primly. "I think I found some keys, but the cars have not been used in quite some time. I have an appointment later this week for a mechanic to come out here and take a look before they're driven anywhere."

"Oh," Cassia said weakly. She wanted to ask about the white car that Sarah drove, the one that had the customized license plate that made it look like a mansion car. She bit her lip to keep herself from saying anything. Tomorrow she would know more. Maybe even tomorrow she would have that white car.

"So there is nothing else?" Sarah asked again, even though she had not really given Cassia much of a chance to speak.

"No, I guess not," Cassia said.

Sarah nodded briskly and turned on her heel to leave.

"Wait," Cassia said, "what exactly does a housekeeper do?"

Sarah tilted her head at the question, and gave a broad smile, the kind Cassia had started to not like very much. "I'd be very happy to answer such an open-ended question, but not at the end of the day. Shall we set up an appointment tomorrow to go over the details?"

An appointment?

"Um, sure," Cassia said. "No, wait, not tomorrow. I have something going on."

Sarah stood, waiting, as if she was fully expecting Cassia to explain in more detail. It took all of Cassia's willpower to not say another word. A jolt of pain ran up her right arm, and she realized she was squeezing the doorknob so tightly that her knuckles shone white.

"I did have one question though," Cassia tried to make a show of looking embarrassed. She was probably a terrible actress. "Have I been getting your name right? Is it Miss Rheton or Mrs. Rheton? I mean, I don't even know if you're married or anything about you, like if you have a boyfriend or a fiancé or something…" Cassia trailed off at the dark look from Sarah.

"Miss, not Mrs." Sarah said, "but thanks for asking. How kind. Tootles." She gave a small wave with her fingertips and turned to go.

She disappeared down the hallway before Cassia realized she had not answered Cassia's question about being married.

Cassia listened at the window she'd cracked open earlier. When she heard the tires of Sarah's car pass over the gravel pad out back and disappear toward the front driveway, she grabbed her copy of *Galactic Dynamics* from the stack of astronomy books on the nightstand, and fanned the pages until the envelope containing the card fell out.

She grabbed her phone and unplugged it from the charger, then sat back on the bed and looked at the card. Tapping on her phone, she looked up the area code: New York. She typed in the whole number, and the search returned: Smith, Chase, Jones, and Associates Law Firm.

A law firm?

Cassia grabbed her backpack from the floor and dug out the will. That was not the law firm listed on the will. So why would someone give her their number? She dialed the number.

A tinny female voice on the other end answered. "Smith,

Chase, and Jones after-hours contact line. Who is your lawyer?"

Cassia tried to think how to respond.

"Hello? Who is your lawyer?" the voice asked again.

"I don't know," Cassia said, deciding the truth was as good as anything else.

"I cannot help you if you do not already have a lawyer on staff."

"I might have a lawyer," Cassia said, bluffing. She had the number after all.

"And who would that be?"

"Um…"

"I need the name of a lawyer at the firm of Smith, Chase, Jones and Associates if I am to help you. Please give me the name of your associate."

"I can't," Cassia said quietly.

"Very well, ma'am. Please call during regular business hours to be on-boarded."

"But—" The line clicked before Cassia could ask… what could she ask? *Hello, person in New York, I might have a lawyer there because some dead person left me your phone number with no explanation and a series of numbers below it that my friend is convinced is a secret code to the mysteries of the universe, but can you please help me anyhow?*

Okay, Genevieve had not said the secrets of the universe, but it wasn't far off from what Genevieve *had* said.

Hello, crazy talk.

She'd have to call back in the morning. There had to be a reason she was given that phone number, and she was going to find out why even if she had to bother every person at that firm.

Slipping the card back into the envelope, she put it back inside the textbook. No one outside of an astrophysics student was going to be looking through a book called Galactic Dynamics, not unless they had some random hobby that involved calculating the speed of stars cruising through the ether.

While she hadn't found her pajamas yet, she had found her favorite slippers—fuzzy orange ones with stars and moons embroidery decorations and a crescent moon hanging by a string from the top of each one. Ted had called her crazy lady when she brought them home from the dollar store, but she didn't care. It had been the best find of the spring. And she needed a win after getting a B in old Greenfellows' quantum mechanics class winter quarter. It hadn't mattered that it was one of the highest grades in the class, it had irked her to no end to not get an A from that crabby old guy from England. Spring quarter she did get an A. She patted the slippers resting on the bed next to her. She thought of them as good luck slippers.

Time for some good luck.

Slipping on the fuzzy orange footwear, Cassia opened the door to the rest of the mansion. As usual, Sarah had turned off nearly all the lights on her way out the door, leaving the place dark and creepy. No matter how many times Cassia said it was okay to leave more lights on, this had always been the result. After the first few days she hadn't bothered making the request anymore.

She padded her way to the kitchen. Popping open the fridge, she pulled out sandwich fixings. Who knew that pimento loaf was addicting? Miss Mansfield followed her into the kitchen, jumped up on a stool by the kitchen island and surveyed Cassia's work.

One mustardy sandwich and a cup of hot cocoa later, Cassia sat on the counter and thought about the numbers on the card. She looked at them so many times, she'd memorized them. Three sets of three numbers. Why did they look so familiar?

She pulled open one drawer after another until she found

one that had a few pens and some paper inside. Grabbing a pen and a slip of paper, she wrote out the three separate groups of numbers.

$$299 \ 792 \ 458$$

None of them were prime numbers. One wasn't the sum of the other two, or any other easy to identify relationship.

It had been a long time since she'd had a lock requiring a code, but those old-fashioned combination locks were usually two digits per position, not three.

Cassia rested her head in her hands, pulling at her hair with her fingers while she stared at the numbers.

It was possible she'd misremembered them. Getting up from the island, she shuffled back to the bedroom, grabbed the book off the nightstand and brought it back to the kitchen. Letting it fall open in front of her on the counter, she pulled out the envelope and removed the card. There were the numbers, just as she'd written them down on the piece of paper.

Except they were written close together with commas between: 299, 792, 458.

What if instead of three numbers, it was one number? Two hundred and ninety-nine million something. Three times ten to the eight.

Cassia's mouth dropped open. She shoved her used sandwich plate away and then pulled the book closer. Flipping through the pages, she scanned until she found what she was looking for. Right there in the formula for calculating the red shift of moving galaxies: c. Better known as the speed of light. Better known as three times ten to the power of eight, if you are rounding up, as astrophysicists usually did.

Flipping to the appendix, Cassia checked the value of the

constant where the tome listed the various values as far as they were accurately known.

She put a finger on the page. "There you are."

The speed of light if you weren't rounding up: 299, 792, 458 meters per second. The exact numbers of the card.

Genevieve was right. It was the key to the universe, just not in the way Genevieve had been thinking about.

What on Earth was it supposed to mean to Cassia?

CHAPTER 16

Miss Mansfield rubbed up against Cassia's hand where it rested against Cassia's forehead. She looked up from the kitchen island counter and that confounding note and met the gaze of the feline. "Meow?"

Cassia glanced over the cat's head at the massive black and white clock on the wall the size of a clock in a museum, and probably costing just as much. It was only ten p.m., but she was exhausted. She had fantasies about coming back to the mansion and doing more snooping after returning the truck, but she couldn't face it after staying up nearly all night the previous night.

Gathering up the sandwich fixings she'd pulled out earlier, she shoved them back in the fridge and wiped down the beautiful granite countertop. Flicking off the lights, she walked to look out the window over the sink. A crescent moon shone into the backyard. Cassia waited while her eyes adjusted. She glanced up, then gasped. The stars above filled the sky. So many stars. The brighter swath of the Milky Way cut across the night sky, clearly visible.

That was a sight she'd never seen in LA. That city never

truly got dark, light pouring out from the millions of people who lived and drove and worked there. But here, darkness blanketed the ground and the only light came from the mansion and the moon and stars above. With a partial moon, the stars had a chance to shine.

Maybe having an observatory out here wasn't such a crazy idea after all.

Especially not if their guests were from New York City. That city had to have as much light pollution as Los Angeles, if not more.

Cassia wondered for a moment what it had been like here, to have fancy parties, and visiting professors, and celebrities all come to visit and look at the stars.

Why couldn't she have known Aunt Mildred when she had been alive? Especially with an observatory out here. Her parents had known of Cassia's obsession with stars and galaxies and science since she had been a little girl. Did they want to keep her away from Aunt Mildred, or did they not even know she existed? She should've pressed her parents harder for more information about family when she still had the chance.

To be fair, no one expects to lose their parents early.

As if sensing her mood, Miss Mansfield rubbed up against her legs, her tiny body vibrating with her purrs.

"Okay, let's go to bed," Cassia said, turning away from the window.

She walked through the darkened mansion to her bedroom. A light from the hallway to the front door caught her eye. She went down the hall to investigate. The light came from the second floor, from the direction of the tower. Cassia and Genevieve had never returned to that room. Cassia remembered the open window. She should have shut it days ago.

"One more task before bed," Cassia said. She grabbed the large flashlight Genevieve had left for her in the hallway, just in case. Exploring the mansion with Genevieve had helped calm some of her anxiety about the place, but it didn't hurt to be careful, especially if creatures like raccoons and squirrels might have come in the window.

She climbed the stairs to the second floor, pausing for a moment on the landing to turn back and admire the view of the stars out the window over the door. It wasn't all bad to not have curtains.

Reaching the top of the stairs, she turned left. Light spilled from the staircase at the far end of the hall; the staircase that led to the tower. She padded down the hall, once again marveling at the thickness of the carpet, and now doubly grateful at the muffling it provided. She reached the stairs to the tower and started up them, trying to ignore the growing ball of anxiety in her stomach. She steadied herself on the wall as she climbed the stairs, putting each foot down slowly so as to not make noise. Instead of rushing ahead as she had before, Miss Mansfield now walked alongside her. Cassia was grateful she did not meow.

Cassia peeked around the last curve in the stairwell before the door. It was shut, but light shone under the bottom of the door. Cassia stopped. She held her breath, straining to hear any noise from within the room. Nothing. She crept up the rest of the stairs, hoping there were no loose boards beneath her feet.

She peered under the door as she climbed the stairs, looking for any shadows or movement. All that was visible was the bottom of the white wall just inside the room.

Taking a deep breath, Cassia mounted the last step and stood before the door. She raised the flashlight with her right hand, ready to strike and defend herself, and turned the knob slowly with her left. The handle turned easily, unlatching the door. Cassia let go of the handle and nudged the door to swing in.

She waited.

No sound greeted the intrusion of the door.

Taking a deep breath, Cassia slowly leaned in with her flashlight weapon held high at the ready and peered into the room, ready to jump back and run if she had to.

But there was no need. The room was empty.

In fact, the room was empty of everything but the furniture. All the papers that had been everywhere were gone, leaving only the shelving and the desk and chair.

Cassia walked around the desk and pulled open one of the drawers. Empty.

A chill ran over her. *What is it with this house and the disappearing belongings?*

Cassia stared at her reflection in the window on the far wall. Someone had pulled the window shut and latched it. Was it the same someone who had taken all the papers?

Whoever had been in the room last had forgotten to turn off the light.

Scowling, Cassia surveyed the desolate room, and then turned and flicked off the light on her way out.

———

Cassia floated through space, enjoying her role as the first female astrophysicist to ever visit the second Lagrange point in person, one million miles from the earth. The beautiful and delicate James Webb telescope spread out in front of her like a shimmering metallic sea. It faced the inky blackness of the universe around them and pulled at its secrets. Her sacrifice of going to fix the telescope in person was to be paid off with fame and fortune and unlimited telescope time, the last worth more than the first two put together.

Struggling with the thick spacesuit needed to protect her from the minus 100 degree Celsius void outside, she raised her wrench to adjust a screw on the sail. Instead of the wrench smoothly latching onto the enormous bolt, it slipped and hit a support strut with alarming force and an accompanying loud bam! Horrified, Cassia pulled back the wrench to try again. She tensed all her muscles, but couldn't seem to hold the wrench with the control she wanted. Slowly, she lowered the wrench again to the bolt. Again, it smashed into the bolt, but this time it flew out of her hands and skittered off toward the center of the delicate reflective surface. No! Cassia screamed in her helmet. She pushed off to grab the wrench, but rather than stop it, the inertia of her push sent her and the wrench smashing down into the reflective surface, destroying it with a loud series of crashes. No! Cassia's heart thundered at her first-hand destruction of three decades of work and several billion dollars. She couldn't stop screaming.

Wait, a tiny voice in her head interjected mid-scream, you can't hear noise in space.

No, you can't. Cassia stopped howling into her helmet.

She struggled, fluttering her eyes and forcing her brain to emerge from sleep, finding herself twisted in the covers, grasping a gigantic flashlight, and half smothered under a very warm black cat.

What a horrible and wonderful dream. As if anyone would ever get to go to the James Webb telescope.

Cassia's mouth tasted terrible. Apparently late night snacking led to bad morning mouth.

Bam!

That wasn't a dream.

Bam! Bam!

Cassia groaned.

This was beginning to be a pattern, and she didn't like it.

Carefully moving Miss Mansfield from her shoulder, Cassia untwisted from the covers and got out of bed. Her pink sweat-pants were good enough, but her t-shirt was thin, so she looked around for the bathrobe she'd found yesterday while looking for her pajamas. It was ratty and old, but her parents had given it to her years ago and she would wear it until it was nothing but two strings held together.

Donning her bathrobe and slippers, Cassia grabbed the large flashlight off the bed and went out the door to the front hall.

Bam! Bam! Bam!

"Hold your horses," Cassia called, feeling out of sorts from not enough sleep.

The banging stopped. Cassia shuffled to the peephole, fully expecting Genevieve and her perfect hair framed in it. Instead, a dark blue eye looked at her, topped with an angry looking eyebrow.

Sheriff Andrews.

Cassia jumped back.

This day was starting especially badly.

Taking a deep breath, Cassia braced herself and then opened the door. "Good morning, Sheriff, how can I help you?" she asked, trying to keep her voice pleasant.

Sheriff Andrews took in her outfit. "Are you not up yet?" he asked. He turned to Deputy Chester standing on the front lawn. "She's not up yet." Deputy Chester nodded, but looked down and refused to meet Cassia's eyes.

"Is that an official question?" Cassia asked Sheriff Andrews, taken aback by his inquiry.

He swung back around to face her. "It's after ten, young lady."

Cassia stared at him. She could think of a few things to say in response, but wasn't going to try her luck with a tall, generally crabby man with a badge and a gun. So instead she came up with the great retort of, "So?"

Which actually worked pretty well, as far as retorts go. The man opened and closed his mouth a few times. It took all of

Cassia's self-control to not smirk. Deputy Chester didn't hide his smile.

Sheriff Andrews finally got his brain working again. "We have a work ethic in this town."

"I'm not working."

That did not go over well either. Cassia tried to soften it. "Not yet, anyhow. I was up late studying." She cleared her throat. "Anyhow, how can I help you now that I am up?"

"We need you to come in for some questions," he said.

"Okay. You could have called." Cassia yawned, swiftly covering her mouth with her hand.

"We did. Many times."

"Oh." Cassia felt in her robe pockets, but her phone wasn't there. She must have left it back in the room. "My cell phone?"

"And the mansion phone."

Cassia jerked her head at that. "The mansion has a phone? I've never seen one."

He narrowed his eyes at her.

"Look, I'm not trying to be difficult, but this place is strangely empty of a lot of things that seem like they should be here…" She trailed off at his glare. He really didn't believe her.

"Which is why I stopped by," he continued, as if she hadn't interrupted him. "Seeing no vehicle—"

"You thought I'd run," she said, completing his sentence. "I told you, I had to return the van."

"How did you get back here?"

"I had a ride."

"From?"

Cassia huffed. "Does it matter?"

"As a matter of fact, it does. I'm placing you under arrest for the murder of Brody Johnson."

"What?" Cassia blurted out, backing up.

He pulled his handcuffs from his belt.

CHAPTER 17

Cassia sat in the oldest jail cell she'd ever seen. It looked like a museum piece, with the old-fashioned bars and hard bench, and even the classic barred windows. They'd even set up an army surplus canvas and wood cot that looked like it had come out of someone's camping setup. The only thing missing was a prime spot on Main Street so she could people watch, or be the entertainment herself, but apparently that didn't make for good tourism, so the jail had been moved back a few blocks from that prime location years ago.

Cassia picked at the muffin and coffee Deputy Chester had gotten her. The muffin was good, but he hadn't gotten her any butter, and apologized profusely for it. That wasn't really the problem, though. It was hard to have an appetite while stuck in jail.

It had taken all of Cassia's convincing to get Sheriff Andrews to at least let her change into a sweater and jeans. Matching her mood, she'd selected an all-black ensemble. Sheriff Andrews had snorted when she came out of the bathroom that Deputy Chester had already inspected to make sure she couldn't escape out a window. Luckily for them, or unluckily for her, the guest bathroom on the first floor didn't have any.

Her one call had been to Nate Perauski. Sheriff Andrews had been kind enough to let her look up his number up in the town phone book, because of course she wasn't allowed to keep her phone, and she didn't have any numbers memorized. After a few minutes of pleading with Mrs. Anderson that indeed it was an emergency, Nate had finally gotten on the line. He said he'd be over later that day as soon as he could wrap up his current business.

Deputy Chester sat at a desk in the front office, just around the corner from the jail cell. Cassia knew because every once in a while he would lean over and peek around the corner and wave at her. She would always wave back. It was beginning to feel like a tradition.

"You doing okay back there, Miss Lemon?"

"I am, Deputy Chester. Is my lawyer here yet?"

"No ma'am. I'll let you know as soon as he gets here."

"Okay, thank you," Cassia said. She shoved the rest of the muffin back in the paper bag and then lay down on the cot. Dust covered the cot and floor of the cell. It smelled musty. Not much business in a small-town jail, she guessed.

Cassia crossed one leg over the other and wiggled her foot with impatience. She'd been planning to call the law firm in New York. It was already past noon, and the day was creeping away.

She'd also wanted to do more exploring in the mansion, to see if there were any more letters for her, or clues like the first one Genevieve had found. Then she'd wanted to visit Genevieve at the diner after her appointment with her lawyer Nate, to see if there was any news on who else could want her out of the mansion.

Instead, she was cooling her heels and contemplating a life in lockup.

Well, at least she'd still have an appointment with Nate, and she didn't even have to ride her bike into town to do it. Of course, making the ride in the back of Sheriff Andrews' squad car was more than a little embarrassing. What seemed like half the town was out in the streets just in time to see her go by sulking in the backseat with Sheriff Andrews and Deputy Chester in the front.

She really was making quite a name for herself in this town.

What really infuriated her was that Sheriff Andrews would not give her any further information except for the name of the victim.

"Did you learn anything else about the person who died?" Cassia had asked on the ride in.

"Not at liberty to say at the moment, ma'am," Sheriff Andrews answered in a terse voice.

"You think that's reasonable?" Cassia asked. "I'm in the back of the squad car because you've arrested me for murder. Don't I have a right to know what I'm charged with?"

He looked at her through the rearview mirror. "I told you what you're charged with. Then I read you your rights."

Cassia glared back at him through the mirror. "You know what I mean," she said.

"Not sure that I do, ma'am," he answered, then turned his eyes to the road, dismissing her.

"It's not ma'am. It's Cassia, Cassia Lemon," Cassia said, her voice breaking with frustration.

He ignored her.

Cassia gave up and turned to face out the window again. A young kid pointed at her as they passed. His mother grabbed the kid's finger and turned them away from staring at Cassia.

Now she was sitting in a jail cell for a murder she supposedly committed less than a day after arriving in town.

Collapsed telescope, murdered person, mansion lost… her

luck was just getting worse, not better. She refused to think of other incidences of bad luck in her life.

She turned to her side and drummed her fingers on the cot.

Deputy Chester leaned around the corner. "You doing okay back there, Miss Lemon?"

"Yes, Deputy Chester, thank you for asking. Is my lawyer here yet?"

"No ma'am. I'll let you know as soon as he gets here."

Deputy Chester leaned back and disappeared from view. Cassia flopped over facedown on the cot, then quickly sat up again in a coughing fit from the dust.

"You okay, Miss Lemon?" Deputy Chester called.

———

The sun was low on the horizon by the time Nate Perauski's massive frame appeared outside the barred walls of her cell, interrupting Cassia's game of shadow puppets on the far wall.

"Sorry it took so long, Miss Lemon," he said, ducking his head. He grabbed one of the bars with his hand, looking like he could have pulled it from the concrete floor. "There isn't a meeting room in this jail. May I come in there?" he asked. Deputy Chester hung behind him, holding a large ring of keys.

Cassia nodded. She smoothed her hair and tried to straighten out the blanket where she'd been laying down.

Deputy Chester inserted a comically old skeleton key into the lock, and turned it, pulling open the door for her lawyer. Nate ducked down nearly a full two feet just to fit through the doorway and then walked to the cot, turned and slowly lowered his body to rest on the rickety wood and canvas. Cassia could have sworn her side of it lifted for a moment before it settled down. She had a momentary vision of being twelve years old playing on the seesaws in the school courtyard.

Once Nate was inside and settled, Deputy Chester locked

the door again. At their looks, he shrugged apologetically. "Rules."

Nate nodded and Deputy Chester went back to the front office.

"The reason it took so long is that I went directly to old Judge Smith's office. He was the one who issued the authority for the arrest. I figured you'd be okay with that, considering how upset you were on the phone that they didn't tell you anything."

Cassia nodded, wanting him to go on.

"They arrested you, because this young man, Brody Johnson, had a piece of paper with your name on it."

"My name?" Cassia asked, touching her chest.

"Yes. Do you, um, did you know this young man?" He watched intently for her answer.

"No, I told you I didn't. I've never seen that kid before in my life," Cassia answered. She hadn't looked at him that closely, but nothing about him had seemed familiar. Certainly not familiar enough for him to have her name.

"Yes, I remember you telling me that. I have to ask, though." Nate cleared his throat. "They are making their case based on the assumption that you two knew each other and it was a deal gone bad."

"Deal? A deal for what?"

"The mansion, perhaps. There were some questions about the fact that no one here in town knew about your existence, and more concerns that your last name does not match the Mandresses."

Yes, Cassia had some of the same questions, but she wasn't going to be putting anyone in jail for them.

"I don't know how he had my name, but I didn't know that guy. Maybe he was stalking me or doing something sketchy and illegal and slipped and fell. I don't see how his knowing me, or knowing of me, proves that I knew him. That's just crazy,"

Cassia said, feeling her throat tighten. She flexed her hands open and shut, trying to will herself to calm down.

Nate flicked his eyes toward the front where Deputy Chester sat out of sight, reminding Cassia that someone was listening to their conversation. Cassia nodded. She looked down and focused on her breathing.

"I had a good discussion with Judge Smith and we've come to an agreement on letting you out on bail, but there is one condition. You have to sign the mansion over as collateral."

"But—" Cassia said.

She was going to mention the probation period for the mansion, but Nate interrupted her, "I know it's a lot, but they are very concerned about your flight risk. No one here knows you." He held up one finger to his lips, signaling to her to not say anything further. She nodded slowly.

"All I need to know for now is do you agree to that for bail, yes or no? We can talk more in my office about the other details." He waited expectantly for her response.

What was the alternative, stay in jail until a trial? Try to raise a ridiculous amount of money some other way. She didn't even want to ask how much bail was. If they wanted the mansion, it was more money than she could get any other way. If she had money, she wouldn't be up in this crazy town trying to survive until she could get into another astronomy graduate PhD program.

Nate waited patiently. His brown eyes watched her. Cassia sighed.

"Yes. I agree," Cassia said.

She put her head in her hands while Nate rose to bang on the bars to get Deputy Chester's attention.

CHAPTER 18

Cassia cradled the steaming cup of decaf coffee while she sat in the hard chair in front of the desk, as Nate, her lawyer, walked around his office, turning on lights. His secretary, Mrs. Anderson, was long gone. They'd walked past her desk on the way in and Cassia marveled at the neatness of every item on it, right down to the dust cover on the electric typewriter. It looked like original equipment.

Nate caught her staring at the typewriter. "It's hers. She brought it in," he said.

"She brought her own typewriter to the job?" Cassia asked.

"It was a condition she had to work here." He gave a small laugh. "Do you think I had an electric typewriter hanging around?"

Good point. It was probably an antique, but then again, so was Mrs. Anderson.

Nate had been kind enough to get her coffee right away. She didn't need caffeine, which would keep her up all night, but something about the warmth and familiar smell helped her feel more settled after her hours spent in the jail.

"Sorry it took so long to get things set," he said. He left his office and went into the reception area, then returned with his own cup of coffee and pulled out the chair behind his desk. Once again, Cassia marveled at his ability to fold his tall body down into the chair and behind the desk.

"Not your fault," she said, and it hadn't been. The sheriff's office had been a little miffed at Judge Smith's agreement to let Cassia out with the mansion as collateral. "This is highly unusual," Sheriff Andrews had said after reading the order from the judge. Cassia had been too tired to even glare at him, instead turning away and waiting patiently for Nate to take care of all the details and call her over for the final signature.

Nate grabbed a coaster and slid it under his coffee cup, then slid one across the desk to Cassia. "So, the evidence they used to get your arrest warrant is circumstantial. If you were a regular resident of this town, I'd wager it wouldn't have been granted."

"Regular?"

"If you had lived here for a while. Generations, to be honest, like most everybody else here. The sheriff made the argument that it was mighty convenient that an heir was found for the mansion when for two decades, or more," Nate gestured at Cassia, "no one has known about your existence. Or of your parents. Do you know your parents' relationship to Mildred Mandress?"

"Just what it said in the will. She was my dad's older sister. I had no idea he had any siblings," Cassia said.

"And you just found out when you got a letter about the mansion?"

Cassia nodded. She took another sip of the coffee, wishing it was a gallon jug of the stuff and she could crawl right in and take a bath. She'd already answered these questions so many times. "I'm sorry. I don't mean to be rude, but I'm really tired. Am I in danger of going to prison, like permanently?"

"Normally, I'd say no, but you don't have an alibi, nor any character witnesses in town."

"But I didn't do anything," Cassia said.

He didn't say anything.

"What can I do about this?" Cassia asked.

"I'm not sure there's anything you can do about this. I will do my best to discourage the sheriff's office and point out that they have to have actual evidence of wrongdoing. Unfortunately, they are under some pressure to find the culprit, if it is murder."

"If it is murder?" Cassia said, perking up. "So they don't know yet, for sure?"

He shook his head. "No, that's what rubbed me wrong about their grabbing you. They're still waiting on a determination from the coroner. Someone had to come up from the Twin Cities special for this, and I hear it took a lot of yelling to get it to happen."

Cassia gripped the coffee tightly, wishing it was Sheriff Andrews' neck. Of all the nerve. It was like he was out to get her or something.

"So it might not be murder, and even if it is, they don't have good evidence against me," Cassia said, listing off the situation.

"All those things are true. That said, it would be much better if strong evidence against the real guilty party was found. A confession would be the best thing of all."

Oh, sure, Cassia could just get that from someone. She groaned.

They sat in silence for a few minutes. Cassia drank her coffee.

"There is something else," Nate said. "I did have time to look into the will for the estate."

Cassia looked up from her cup.

"The will had another executor before the law firm. Rose Johnson."

Cassia nodded. She'd forgotten until now, but there had been something in the first few pages of the mumbo jumbo that was the will document. It also explained why the name Johnson seemed familiar.

"Rose Johnson was the previous housekeeper," Nate continued. "They had the address of the mansion as her official address."

"She lived there?" Cassia asked. Thank goodness Sarah didn't live there now. "What happened?"

"She died a few years back. Apparently, Mildred Mandress did not update her will, or at least didn't file an updated will."

"So, there could be another will out there?"

"Yes, but if no one finds it, then it hardly matters," he said, fiddling with the handle of his empty cup of coffee. "That is how you got a call from the lawyers in California. They were the firm on record in her will. Apparently, they did business with her father years ago and she kept them on. Having no one else suitable, and with your possible conflict of interest, Judge Smith appointed them executors of the will at the county's prompting."

"From California?" Cassia asked. "How could they do that from so far away?"

"Most legal stuff is easy to do, even from out of state," Nate said, trying to assure her.

"But it seems like someone cleaned out the house of all of Aunt Mildred's personal stuff. Do you think they did that, too?"

"From California? I doubt it. Unless they were on retainer ahead of time, it's unlikely they'd fly someone out to take care of such matters. Besides, why remove those items if there was only one beneficiary, and they were to receive the house and contents?" Nate asked.

Good question. But unless Aunt Mildred lived like a minimalist in a museum, her stuff had gone somewhere. Someone took it. Could it be the same person that killed that young guy? Cassia looked into her empty cup as her mind raced with the possibilities. Sarah seemed the most likely suspect. After all, she had the keys and no supervision, or so it seemed.

"That isn't the bad part, or at least I don't think so," Nate said, interrupting Cassia's thoughts.

She set the cup down and looked up at him, waiting.

He opened his mouth to speak, then hesitated.

"What is it?" Cassia said, unable to decipher his expression.

"Brody Johnson was Rose Johnson's grandson.

"The victim?" Cassia said. The room tilted a bit. She shut her eyes and gripped the edge of the chair.

The victim was related to the old housekeeper.

Cassia opened her eyes again and looked up at Nate.

"That's…" Cassia searched for the word. Coincidence seemed too mild.

"Yes," Nate agreed.

"But didn't she die years ago? Why would he be at the house now? Or rather, on the house in a storm?" Cassia asked. She covered her mouth to stop the questions.

"I don't know for most of those questions. Yes, she did die a while ago, which makes it even stranger that Mildred didn't amend her will and name a new executor." Nate leaned in. "I will say finding out the answers to those questions might help you prove your innocence."

Cassia bit her lip.

———

Darkness blanketed main street. Cassia stood bathed in light pouring from the window of the door of the diner. Inside, it was packed. Every booth was taken, every table filled, some tables crammed with additional chairs, making the room look like a sea of people. Even the stools at the bar were full, with additional people standing next to those diners as if they were at a nightclub pushing in to get drinks at the bar. Cassia checked her phone. It was seven p.m. on a Thursday night.

Genevieve had returned her text with another text, telling her to come to the diner. She would give Cassia a ride home after work and Trent said that there was a dinner waiting for her. Cassia didn't even care that they'd ask her a million questions in exchange. The thought of going back to the mansion alone after the day she had was unbearable. So she told Nate that she had a ride home and turned down his offer to run her out to the mansion when he found out that she no longer had her van.

Cassia hesitated outside the diner, though. She thought it would be quiet on a weeknight, and she'd have a relaxing meal with her friends. Instead, it was chaos inside; Many more people were there than had been there the first time she'd come.

Taking a deep breath, she grasped the door handle and pulled. The bells rang just as the warmth and noise and smell of apple pie flowed out over her. The noise quickly silenced as everyone turned to stare at her, and then resumed at a higher volume as people looked away and pretended to not be talking about her.

Wending her way through the crowded dining area, Cassia found an open spot on the counter near the wall. She slid in and gratefully sat on the stool. At the table behind her, a young boy's voice piped up, "there's the bad lady from the cop car." Cassia almost laughed out loud, despite herself. She turned around to give the big boy a smile and watch his mother's embarrassed red face as she tried to hush her son. Cassia waved at them, leaning into the awkward moment.

"Girl, I saw that," Genevieve said as she slid a hot cider

with a cinnamon stick coming out of it across the counter to Cassia. Turning back to face the counter, Cassia gave her friend a smile as she gratefully accepted the drink.

"As if that's even close to the worst thing that happened to me today," Cassia said.

The dark look passed over Genevieve's face. "True. And I want to hear all about it, but I have to get through this dinner rush first."

"It's a Thursday night. Why are there so many people here?" Cassia asked.

"It's our answer to the Friday night fish frys. Thursday steak night."

"Doesn't have quite the same ring," Cassia said.

"No, it doesn't," Genevieve said, giving a nod, "but it is very popular. Plus we also do the fish frys. We give a deal to come to both in one week. What can I getcha?"

Cassia saw a laminated menu stuck in the condiment tray one seat over, and started to grab it when she saw Genevieve's look and pulled her hand back. "I'll guess I'll go for—"

"Chef's choice," Genevieve said, completing the sentence with Cassia. "Good girl. You're a quick learner."

"I am, and I like delicious food."

"You and the rest of the town," Genevieve said, wiping down the counter in front of Cassia.

Cassia glanced back at the patrons. "Is this everyone who lives in town?"

"Most of them. The ones behind you, with the boy pointing out your jailbird status, are the Smiths."

"The Smiths of the party-at-the-mansion fame?" Cassia asked, teasing Genevieve. She turned around to face the table behind her. The boy was staring at her with big, round, blue eyes. Cassia got the impression he had been staring at her the whole time. She gave the group another smile and a wave, and this time called out, "Sorry to ruin your party. Maybe I can make it up to you sometime with a party of my own."

The adults at the table stared at her, their mouths hanging slightly open. The young boy grabbed his mother's sleeve and tugged hard and said, "She's gonna have a party." His mother clasped his hand and pulled it away from her sleeve without breaking her stare at Cassia.

Genevieve poked Cassia in the back. "Are you nuts?"

Cassia turned back around to face Genevieve, who looked less than amused. "Sorry. It's been a day."

"I can see that. Just sit here and wait for your food, and don't make any more friends."

Cassia snorted, then drank half of her cider. "Okay, but only if I get another one of these."

Genevieve swiped the mug away from Cassia. "Fine. Behave."

Cassia shrugged her shoulders.

Genevieve walked away.

Cassia twisted in her seat so her back was to the wall. She sipped the water Genevieve had brought along with the cider and tried to inconspicuously look at all the patrons. Now she was regretting coming in the front door so fast. She could have stared in from the dark outside.

One of these people might have been the one to come and kill that kid at the mansion, if indeed his death was a murder. And more than one of them could want her gone. She was a stranger, after all—one who'd gone and inherited the biggest property around. Nate had told her that the mansion came with a huge plot of land that was probably worth more than the building itself, which boggled Cassia's mind. The will hadn't really made that clear, or at least for her in what little she could understand of it.

"How did you get that?" she'd asked him when he'd pulled out the huge printout of the plot of land.

"Public county records."

Oh. Why hadn't she thought of that?

"See that line?" He pointed to a section of land midway between the mansion and downtown Forgotten Valley.

"Yes?"

"That was where they split off the original plot. It used to be much bigger."

Cassia's eyes rounded. It was huge now. "What happened?"

"They gave this section," he pointed to Forgotten Valley, "to the county in exchange for special tax status on the rest of the land. In perpetuity. "

"Perpe...What does that mean?"

"Forever."

"What status?" Cassia asked.

"Tax free, pretty much. The property, the land, the lumber on the land. No taxes. Ever. Helluva way to prepay them."

"As long as the county doesn't change the rules," Cassia added.

"Aren't you a little young to be so jaded?" Nate asked with a small laugh.

"A lot's happened."

He hadn't asked for clarification, and Cassia hadn't volunteered any.

Now she was in this town and sitting on the most prime real estate around. She'd want it too, if she was them.

She looked around the place, stymied. What would a murderer look like anyhow? She had no idea. Here, families with small kids, old folks, and a few younger people in flannel and jeans filled out the diner. No one wore a sign that said 'murderer here.'

Cassia's stomach rumbled. It was not concerned with the folks in the diner at the moment.

Just in time, Genevieve came back along the back of the

counter, carrying a huge tray. Cassia twisted back to face the counter.

"Here girl, this should improve your mood," Genevieve said as she unloaded a plate of meatballs over veggies and a side of pasta in a garlic sauce. A creamy chocolate dessert came with it.

"Meatballs on a steak night?" Cassia asked.

"Steak meatballs," Genevieve said. At Cassia's puzzled look, she only said, "Trust me."

The smell convinced Cassia in less than a second. She barely heard Genevieve's "We'll talk in a bit," before she bit into a piece of heaven.

CHAPTER 19

Genevieve locked the front door of the empty diner. Trent came out from the back with the steaming pitcher of mulled cider and three glasses. He and Jack, his kitchen help, had cleaned the kitchen while Genevieve and Cassia cleaned the dining room. Cassia hadn't minded the physical work of mopping and wiping counters after sitting around all day.

"No Jack tonight?" Genevieve asked Trent.

"He had to go. Something about running to a lumber-yard." Trent set the glasses down at a booth and poured out the cider. He held up one glass to Cassia, and she walked over and accepted it. "Sit. I heard you had quite the day."

"Yes," she said. She slid into the booth, making room for Genevieve to come sit next to her. Once they were all settled, Trent and Genevieve looked at Cassia expectantly. "Now?"

They both nodded.

She told them about the arrest and what Nate had told her about the property. Trent whistled a low whistle when she mentioned the tax status. "What I wouldn't give for that," he said.

When Cassia finished, she searched their eyes. "So, who do

you think would have something out for the housekeeper's grandson?"

Genevieve laughed. "Don't you think you're skipping ahead a bit?"

"What do you mean?" Cassia asked.

"Well, if his grandmother died two years ago, what was he doing out at the estate? That might be the question to start with."

Trent leaned in to get their attention. "Especially if he had your name on him. How did he know you?"

Cassia thought for a minute. "I have no idea. But that's why the sheriff's office thought I was somehow involved. They don't believe me when I say I didn't know him."

"This sucks," Genevieve said. "Today, I mean, besides the arrest, you've got nothing but more questions and no answers."

"I did learn about the property," Cassia said.

"True," Trent said, "and the land."

"And the land," Cassia said.

Trent tapped his fingers on his mug, then stopped and stared at Cassia. "Wait, what happens to the property if you don't meet the conditions of the will? Was that spelled out?"

Trent and Genevieve looked at Cassia like she should know the answer.

Maybe she should.

Cassia ducked her head down, frustrated. "I don't know," Cassia said. "The will just said I wouldn't have it. Do you think there's another part of the will that I didn't get to see? Or there's some law about that..."

Why hadn't Nate said anything about that part?

"I dunno," Genevieve said, "it seems the number one suspect would be whoever would inherit it if you can't."

That made sense.

———

Cassia stretched, careful not to spill a cup of coffee in her right hand. She turned her face to the sun and enjoyed its midmorning shine, allowing it to warm her in addition to the coffee. She stood on the front lawn of the mansion, the door behind her open and Miss Mansfield stood just inside it. Not a cloud ruined the blue sky overhead, and birds were singing in the trees.

Despite everything that happened yesterday, Cassia couldn't help but enjoy the beautiful morning. She'd slept in as late as she wanted. Nothing had disturbed her. No banging on the doors. No phone calls. No arrest warrants. She had a lot to take care of, but for at least this one morning everything was perfect.

She turned back to the black cat. "What do you think, Miss Mansfield? Is this a perfect day or what?"

Miss Mansfield yawned, her needle white teeth showing crisply against her pink mouth and black fur.

"I agree," Cassia said, "but it's too beautiful to go back to sleep. Besides, I have much to do if I want to stay here and enjoy more of these days."

Unimpressed, Miss Mansfield turned and walked back deeper into the mansion.

Cassia walked to the front steps and sat in a sunny spot, cradling her cup. As soon as she finished her coffee and ate some breakfast, she'd get dressed and grab her bike and go exploring. It was a long shot, but maybe she could learn something by checking out her neighbors. Plus, it would feel good to get outside.

Half an hour later, Cassia changed out of her sweats into some jeans, a t-shirt, and a hoodie for the day. She grabbed her phone off the cardboard box that was doubling as her desk in the bedroom and checked again for any calls or messages she missed while outside. Her battery was starting to go, and she'd forgotten to plug it in last night, so she was trying to get more juice before she went on her bike ride.

No calls, but a quick glance at her call log reminded her that she needed to call the law firm in New York while they were still open. Hitting redial, the phone rang a strange tone that reminded Cassia of the old movies from the nineteen thirties.

"Smith, Chase and Jones, how may I direct your call?" a young man asked on the other end of the line.

"I'm not sure," Cassia said. "I had this phone number left for me by someone…" Cassia hesitated. How weird was it to say the number was left by a deceased relative?

"For a new case, or for something else?" the young man asked.

"Probably for something else," Cassia said.

The line was quiet for a second.

"Did they leave you any other information about why they left the number?" he asked, mild exasperation in his tone.

"There was a nine digit code," Cassia said. "Do you have files by case numbers?"

"No, generally not given to the clients, anyway. Is there a name associated with this that I can try to look it up with?"

"Cassia Lemon. No, wait, it might be under Mildred Mandress. Or her father. I don't know his first name." Cassia's face warmed at her lack of preparation. Why didn't she get his name before calling? It couldn't have been hard, especially since they were related.

"Can you hold the line for a moment?" he asked.

"Yes," Cassia answered. She sat down heavily on her bed and listened to the elevator music version of pop songs they had for their hold music. Somehow she had expected jazz.

A moment later he returned, his tone now brisk. "Ma'am—"

"Cassia."

"Um, Cassia, can I get a number to call you back? A few of our partners are out today, so I'm not able to look up this information at the moment. We'll call you back as soon as we can."

"Okay. When might that be?" Cassia asked. "I think it might be important."

"I understand. However, I'm unable to help you at the moment. I'll take this information and give it to the right people when they return. We're not blowing you off," he said.

"Okay," Cassia said. She hung up, feeling very much blown off.

Cassia carried her bike out from the back hallway where she'd stashed it. Finding her bike's air pump and topping off her tires had mollified some of her disappointment at failing to get more information from the law firm. At least she'd remembered to call.

Outside, some puffy clouds had encroached on the perfect blue sky, but it was still nice out. Cassia locked the front door behind her and stashed the keys in her backpack, along with her phone, and put it on. It was almost eleven a.m., and true to form, Sarah was not there yet. Cassia dreaded the conversation they were going to have about that.

Cassia pulled on her bike helmet and snapped the buckle underneath her chin. She felt ridiculous wearing it, but after seeing one particularly bad accident on campus where a student had met a bad end thanks to a car, she never skipped it.

Thankfully, she had a mountain bike because that was what was most common on campus, and had been the easiest for her to buy secondhand. It would come in handy riding over the rough ground and the gravel driveway of the mansion.

Out of curiosity, she pedaled toward the back of the building, in the direction of the garage in the woods. She might have missed something when she had driven the van back there. It had been dark.

Everything looked the same as when she had first seen it in the headlights of the van: the collapsed and empty shed, the gravel pad full of weeds, the scraggly trees and bushes behind the addition with the observatory. She biked back through the woods to the four car garage. All the doors of the building were shut. She biked up to the long side windows and stood on her pedals to peer inside while balancing herself with one hand on the garage. The white car was gone, but everything else looked the same.

Cassia pushed away from the garage and started riding away when a large boom rang out through the trees and shook the air. She nearly fell off her bike and skidded to a rough stop, hopping on one foot to keep from tipping over. Leaves trickled down from the trees.

Another boom followed. More leaves fell.

Cassia got off her bike. The noise was coming from deeper in the woods, past the garage. From Nate's map yesterday, all that land back there for miles and miles belonged to the mansion. There should be nothing going on back there.

A third boom rang out. Two crows flew overhead away from the direction of the noise, complaining loudly. Cassia felt they had the right of it.

She held on to the bike and looked back at the mansion. Between the trees, it looked exactly the same. No cars were coming up the drive. She only expected Sarah, but the housekeeper was probably not going to make an appearance for another hour or more.

A fourth, not quite as loud, boom rang out, this time followed up with the high-pitched whine of a chain saw. Cassia's head whipped around to look back at the woods. Someone was using a chain saw in her woods.

Getting off, she walked the bike over to the garage and

leaned it up against the side, then started to the woods. Reconsidering, she went back and moved the bike to the back of the garage. This way Sarah would not see the bike when she came to work. Perhaps that wasn't the right choice, but Cassia didn't know if she could trust the housekeeper. If Cassia was going to go sneaking in the woods, she didn't want Sarah sneaking up behind her.

She hung her helmet on the handlebars, then pulled her jacket out of her backpack and put on the light nylon garment. It was cool in the woods.

Cassia walked into the trees in the direction of the noises, scanning ahead as she carefully stepped through the dead leaves and small branches on the forest floor. The smaller trees of the edge of the wood gave way to larger, thicker trunks. The walking grew easier as the brush thinned underneath the thick canopy overhead, but that meant there were fewer places to hide.

Finally, she spied movement in the distance accompanying another loud boom. A large tree slowly fell, the tangle of its upper branches with its neighbors only slightly slowing its fall. Behind it, a large yellow truck on caterpillar treads swung its claw around and grabbed the trunk of the tree, while another truck with massive wheels and a metal front assembly backed up from its position after having pushed over the tree.

Cassia stopped.

That tree was huge.

Which meant those pieces of equipment were even larger.

This wasn't someone poaching a tree here or there, it was a full-scale operation. Part of her knew that already from the number of large crashes and booms she'd heard walking out to the location, but it was another thing to see it laid out in front of her.

Her hands curled into fists.

Not only were these people destroying this lovely wood, they were stealing from her.

She wanted to yell and kick them off the property, but she could see three trucks, and who knew how many people over there with chain saws. If they were doing something illegal, they sure as heck were not going to be happy to see her, nor likely to get when she told them to go.

Cassia wondered what Mr-follow-the-rules Sheriff Andrews would say about all this. Calling the sheriff's office was the smartest thing to do, but she had no idea exactly where she was or who those people were.

Unhooking her backpack from one shoulder, Cassia swung it around and pulled out her cell phone. She turned on the location services for her photographs and then took a picture of the machines working. There was probably a much better way to figure out her GPS location, but she wasn't going to fiddle with it now to find out.

The photo itself looked terrible. It looked like a bunch of trees. The yellow machinery blended in with the leaves and debris, leaving it hard to see. That was what she got for being a poor student who couldn't afford the newest of new smart phones.

Worse, it was absolutely impossible to pick out the people. She could just see Sheriff Andrews' sneer when she asked him to do something about it. She would bet a donut he'd say something like, "What, you want me to go arrest the trees?"

There was no use for it but for her to get closer for better photos.

Cassia hesitated. Whoever this was in her woods was probably not the happy-to-see-visitors type. She looked down at the fuzzy photo. Zooming in on the truck in the photograph, she could just barely make out that there was a company name printed on the side, but it was too fuzzy for her to read it.

Another tree went down. Cassia's anger at the destruction was enough to push her forward. How very dare they.

She changed the setting on her phone camera to video so she wouldn't have to mess with the shutter when trying to get closer. Holding up the camera, she ran from tree to tree, filming between, but otherwise ducking low and trying to stay out of sight until she got safely behind another tree.

It was only when she got within hearing distance of the workers did she realize her mistake; the reflective stripes she'd taped on her jacket for visibility last year, and forgotten about, didn't blend in with the woods. A worker must have spotted her when the light hit her jacket on one of her dashes because he yelled an alarm.

Seconds later, a shot rang out and bounced off of the tree Cassia was hiding behind.

CHAPTER 20

Cassia panted against the tree, her heart racing in her ears. She grabbed at the rough bark and tried to think with the adrenaline shooting through her.

They had shot at her!

As if it was in slow motion, she watched the piece of bark blown off the tree fall to the ground.

More yells came from the work site.

The trucks quieted as they stopped pushing and lifting the trees, but the engines didn't cut off.

On the other side of the tree where Cassia hid, smaller sticks broke and running footsteps disturbed the detritus on the forest floor. The noise echoed in the trees.

At least one logger, if not more, was running into the woods looking for her.

Cassia looked down at the loam at her feet. She dropped and scrabbled, pushing aside the dead leaves, looking for rocks, anything.

No luck.

Digging her fingers into the moist and heavy earth, she grabbed a clump, and whipped it in the direction away from the mansion. It disturbed the branches of a scraggly bush as it fell, looking like it could have been her running away.

A shot rang out after it.

Cassia crouched low and ran in the other direction. She pulled off her backpack while running and held on to one of its straps with one arm while wiggling and pulling off her jacket. She tripped over a root and wiped out, sliding in the dirt and leaves down a small slope. At the bottom, she shoved her jacket under a pile of leaves and got back to her feet and ran.

The noise behind her grew louder. They must have figured out that she hadn't gone the other way.

She scrambled some more, running and tripping as she went.

This was no good. She probably couldn't outrun them.

Up ahead, the trees were larger and spaced further apart. She had to find a hiding spot, and soon. If they got close behind her, they'd see her for sure.

She picked a spot and ran as fast as she could, counting in her head the way she always did when stressed.

———

After what felt like an hour of not hearing any pursuers, Cassia thought it safe to peek out from the center of the dead tree she'd scrambled inside. Dampness soaked through her jeans and shirt. It made her think of bugs and other creatures that lived in dead and decaying things. Her skin crawled at the thought.

Her hand gripped the edge of the shell of the enormous tree and she pulled herself out of its rotten center. It smelled like mushrooms, and not the fresh kind. After extracting herself, she wiped off her jeans and shirt. It didn't do much good.

She pulled her backpack out from the bottom of the dead tree. Luckily, she'd zipped it far enough shut that her phone and keys were still inside. A crack ran across the screen of her phone, but she could still read it, and it was still on. No signal. She'd have to get closer to the mansion or to town to make a call.

A twenty minute run later, she was back at the mansion. No construction noises sounded through the woods. That just made Cassia more nervous. Those people could be anywhere.

Her bike was where she'd left it. Cassia peeked inside the garage. No white car, so no Sarah yet either. Cassia walked her bike back to the front of the mansion, then brought it in and locked the door. She wedged a wood chair under the handle.

A short shower and clean clothes later, she sat in her room, staring at her phone. Being in the mansion alone felt like being a sitting duck waiting for the hunters to arrive. Much as Sarah got on Cassia's nerves, she found herself wishing the house-keeper was there.

Cassia pulled up Sheriff Andrews' number on her phone and placed her finger on the screen to dial, then stopped. The man already seemed like he hated her. Convincing him of a problem could be difficult over the phone, especially since she couldn't show him the photographs and video on her phone. She could though if she talked to him in person. Plus, if she went into town, she might be able to sneak in a conversation with Nate about who got the house if she bombed out on the conditions of the will without him running his very expensive meter up for the privilege.

The problem was getting downtown. She'd returned the van, and Sarah still had not given her a set of keys to any of the cars out back. Genevieve was working and couldn't come get her, and Cassia didn't want to bother Nate for that. She wasn't going to pay his hourly for a ride into town.

The only thing left was walking or her bike.

Cassia pulled on an old brown zip up hoodie, then grabbed her charger and damaged phone and shoved them into her old messenger bag and slung it across her body. She went into the kitchen and set out three bowls of food for Miss Mansfield and several dishes of water. The feline stared at her balefully.

"I'm sorry, I'm sorry... I probably won't be long, but just in case," Cassia said.

That didn't even earn an eye blink from the cat.

"I promise."

Miss Mansfield turned her back on Cassia to lay in her bed in the kitchen.

Giving up, Cassia grabbed her bike from the hall and went to the front door. She peeked out the peephole and then looked out the front parlor windows for good measure. No one was outside. Taking a deep breath, she moved the chair from under the front door handle and unlocked the door and rolled her bike outside. After locking the door behind her, she mounted her bike and started the long ride into town.

Downtown Forgotten Valley lay about twenty miles as the crow flies from the mansion. Unfortunately, the road didn't care much for how crows traveled, and it twisted and turned, adding a handful of miles to the trip. Cassia didn't know which she hated more, the sections of road that passed through thick patches of trees that could hide any count of people with guns, or the parts that passed through long crop fields, leaving her exposed for all to see. She hunched down low on the handle-bars and pedaled as fast as she could.

Clouds had come in to cover the sky while Cassia was showering, giving the day a gray overcast feel. It matched her mood perfectly. She'd never been shot at. Another new experience in Forgotten Valley.

Frankly, she'd had enough of new experiences.

A handful of cars passed Cassia. Her heart raced with each one. Her plan was to ride into the ditch and try to hide there if a construction vehicle came by. Thankfully, she didn't have to try that plan out. She topped the last hill and looked down on downtown Forgotten Valley. A small tourist town never looked so good.

———

Cassia stood in front of Deputy Chester in the front office of the jail. She shoved her hands into her pockets to keep herself from crossing her arms and further putting the deputy's back up. He shifted uneasily from one leg to the other, while gingerly holding her phone in his right hand and scrolling with his left to look at all the pictures. Cassia focused on her breathing and the pattern on the linoleum floor to distract herself from the agonizing slowness of his examination of the evidence.

Today the smell of dust and stale muffins in the office was only annoying, and not as depressing as it had been yesterday when she'd been behind bars. The sun was not yet streaming in, as it would later in the day, leaving the office dark and cool. Sheriff Andrews was nowhere to be seen.

"Ma'am—" Deputy Chester began.

"Cassia," Cassia said.

"Miss Lemon," he said, stealing a glance at her. She nodded back. "Miss Lemon, owning the land does not necessarily mean that you own the trees on it. What they are doing could be perfectly legal."

"That doesn't make any sense," Cassia said, protesting. "Could they come digging for whatever they want within the soil, too?"

"Possibly," a deep voice said from behind Cassia. She turned. Sheriff Andrews stood in the doorway from the street. Cassia had not even heard him open the door.

"What?" Cassia asked.

"It's called mineral rights. You have to check your deed," Sheriff Andrews said. He came into the office and joined them.

Cassia hated having to look up at him, especially now that he seemed so smug. Plus, it was horrifying to hear that she might not have any control over this property she supposedly inherited.

"What's going on?" Sheriff Andrews asked, turning to Deputy Chester.

It took all of Cassia's willpower not to throw up her hands at being bypassed for information.

"She says there was logging on her property," Deputy Chester said, indicating the phone.

"So?" Sheriff Andrews said to Cassia. "Do you know the terms of your deed? Do you have the timber rights?"

Cassia opened her mouth to speak and then shut it again. She did not know what timber rights were, much less if she had them. Sheriff Andrews' expression turned into something infuriatingly like a smirk.

Turning to Deputy Chester, Cassia put out a hand for her phone. He handed it over with a nod and backed up a step, as if trying to get out from between her and Sheriff Andrews.

Cassia scrolled through the phone until she found the video clip at the end. She hit play, then held up the phone screen to Sheriff Andrews and waited. At first only the sound of her running and the background noise of the machinery came from the tinny speakers. After several minutes, the worker's shout echoed and then the unmistakable sound of a bullet ricocheting off a tree trunk came out of the phone.

Sheriff Andrews raised both eyebrows.

"They shot at me," Cassia said.

"Could be hunting," Deputy Chester said, piping in from the side.

Cassia and Sheriff Andrews both turned to Deputy Chester.

A million questions ran through Cassia's head, but the first one that came out of her mouth was "Is it hunting season?"

Deputy Chester slowly shook his head, then looked down and backed away.

"See, it's not hunting season," Cassia said to Sheriff Andrews. "And I wouldn't give permission if it was."

"Is your land posted with no trespassing and no hunting signs?" Sheriff Andrews asked her.

"I don't know," Cassia said.

"Then you might have given permission," Sheriff Andrews said.

"Is it ever legal to hunt humans?" Cassia retorted.

It was silent in the office for a minute.

Sheriff Andrews broke it. "They probably thought you were a deer."

Cassia gave in to her inner frustration and folded her arms and glared back at him. "Not… hunting… season."

CHAPTER 21

"Hello, Mrs. Anderson," Cassia said, giving the secretary a small wave. The secretary stopped typing on her electric typewriter and looked up, peering at her through the dust motes floating in the empty law office waiting room. Her beehive seemed even higher than last time. Cassia wondered if it would be possible to hide a puppy inside of it. Probably a chihuahua.

"Is Mr. Perauski in? I just have a quick question or two," Cassia said. After her less than successful encounter at the sheriff's office, she thought it would be a good idea to get some more information about the property. Luckily, Nate's law office was just two blocks away. Or several decades, if one went by his secretary.

Mrs. Anderson wrinkled her nose at Cassia. "Yes, but he's busy."

"It'll only take a minute," Cassia said. "I would have called, but I was downtown already."

Before Mrs. Anderson could say anything, Nate Perauski appeared in the doorway to the inner office. "It's fine, Deloris," he said to Mrs. Anderson, then waved Cassia back to his office.

"You're back so soon. Did something happen?" he asked.

Cassia nodded, then explained about the incident in the wood and her aggravating discussion with Deputy Chester and Sheriff Andrews. "I don't remember anything in the will about separate rights."

"Nor do I," Nate said. "Wills are not always as precise as one might hope for."

"Then where can I get this information?" Cassia said, cutting him off in her eagerness.

"The original deed is on file with the county. If any rights were sold, they should be filed with the county as well. Did you get any more information or paperwork from the law firm that's acting as executor?"

Cassia shook her head. "I get the feeling that they're waiting for me to make it through the probationary period before doing too much work."

"And you haven't found any information on the property itself? In an office? Locked away in a box?" Nate asked. "Most houses have a paper deed, but often they're lost over the years. Of course, that's no guarantee any rights sales would be with the original document."

"That's the thing," Cassia said, "I haven't found any papers with the house. It's like a hotel or something. There're no personal goods in it at all."

Nate leaned back in his chair and tented his fingers, staring thoughtfully across the desk. "Yes, you mentioned that. Very strange."

It was very strange. Now, worse, it could be dangerous if all sorts of people had rights to the land she didn't know about. Plus, if there was a document listing the timber rights sales to another party, it might be the quickest way to find out who shot at her.

"I need to find out for sure about those rights," Cassia said. "Because if those people were poaching and actually shooting at me and not mistaking me for a strange deer with reflective tape on its nylon jacket, then they would be the obvious suspects for wanting me gone. It's not that far from hanging a kid off the roof to shooting someone else in the woods."

Nate sat up. "Good point." He checked his watch. "I won't be able to make it down to the county offices before they close today, but I can go first thing in the morning. They are open a half day on Saturday mornings. I can get that information right away and give you a call. Let me get your number again, so I don't have to get it out of the files."

Cassia nodded. "None of that information's online?" she asked, as she scribbled her phone number on a pad he had pushed toward her.

"Some, depending on the year filed, but I think in this case it's worth the trip to make sure I get all the records," Nate said.

Cassia had to agree with that. She put the pen down. "There's one other thing, who gets the house, I mean the mansion and stuff, if I don't live out my probationary year in it and get a job in town?"

He stared at her. "I thought you knew. If you don't pass your probationary period, the property goes to the state."

Well, that narrows it down, Cassia thought glumly.

———

Cassia made her way down Main Street to the diner, pushing her bike as she walked. It was early afternoon and most people were still at work, leaving the streets empty. A deeper gray tinged the low clouds to the west, and the air smelled of rain. She hoped she wouldn't have to ride home in a storm.

Her stomach growled. Breakfast was a long time ago. In her rush to talk to the sheriff and Nate, she'd skipped lunch and her body was letting her know that was not an okay plan.

She pulled the U-lock out of its bracket and locked her bike to a parking meter. Hopefully that was not against Sheriff

Andrews' rules, too. She wasn't in the mood to see him again today.

The bells rang as Cassia opened the door to the diner.

Genevieve sat at one table with a pile of napkins and a tray of silverware in front of her, rolling bundles for the night's rush. Trent and Jack yelled in the back, and banged around in the kitchen, probably preparing for that night's fish fry.

Genevieve got up when Cassia entered. "Good, you're here," Genevieve said, then pulled the door shut and locked it behind her.

At Cassia's stare, Genevieve explained, "We're not open right now, so you're technically not a customer." She patted Cassia on the shoulder and pushed her to one of the open tables. "One of the perks of preFriday fish fry madness is staff gets time to prepare. I'll be right back."

Cassia obediently sat. She knew better than to ask for a menu.

Genevieve brought a water over for Cassia before going to the swinging partition that separated the dining area from the kitchen and speaking over it to Jack and Trent.

"Food's coming," Genevieve said as she sat down next to Cassia. "So, what's up? You sounded upset."

Cassia drank half her water, then launched into the morning's events, Genevieve's eyes growing wider with each new thing.

"Can I see the photos?" Genevieve asked after Cassia had wound down with the last details from her visit to the lawyer.

Cassia nodded.

"Oh, wait a minute," Genevieve said, then retrieved Cassia's lunch that had just appeared in the kitchen window. She came back with a dish loaded with fried fish, fries and coleslaw and set it down in front of Cassia, along with a set of condiments. "Pie later."

Cassia unlocked her phone, opened it to the recent photos

and videos, and gladly handed it over so she could eat. It was all hot and fresh. For a brief wonderful moment, her problems disappeared in the heady taste of hot and crunchy fish fillets.

———

Genevieve zoomed in on one of the pictures. "This logo looks familiar."

Cassia looked up. She put a hand over her mouth and forced herself to swallow before speaking. "Really? None of it looked familiar to me."

"We have a lot of family businesses around here. I bet someone would know who this is."

"But would they help me?" Cassia asked, the words coming up before she thought about them.

"Not everyone around here is terrible," Genevieve said, lowering the phone and staring at Cassia.

"Sorry. I'm a little bitter. Someone shot a gun at me today," Cassia said. She concentrated on her plate. She knew she was acting sullen, but after her morning it seemed reasonable.

"Point," Genevieve said. "But I know of at least one trust-worthy person—" she waved at Cassia's look, "—in addition to my coworkers at the diner."

Genevieve paused dramatically.

"Okay, I'll bite, who?" Cassia said.

"Roger. Remember, I told you he might accidentally on purpose take a photo for us? Look, he is the best handyman in three counties, and he barely charges for his work, except in strange food. I bet you there's not a business around he has not done some work for. He could probably tell you exactly who this company is, and where they're located. He could probably tell you about each of those individual trucks." Genevieve pointed to the cell phone photo and laughed.

"Really?" Cassia hesitated.

"I know what you're thinking," Genevieve said.

Cassia raised her eyebrows at Genevieve.

"Can you trust him? I'm telling you, you can. He's a good person. When I came back to help my mom when she was sick, he would always help us out with our terrible apartment, no matter how tight things were for money, just telling us to get him later when we could. He does that for lots of folks, which is partly why the diner is so careful to always pay, and right away."

A knot in Cassia's chest loosened. The first good news she'd heard all day. "When can we talk to him?" Cassia asked.

"How about tonight?" Genevieve said. "We could find out who the company is right away and be ready if your lawyer comes back and says they have no rights."

That would be as soon as tomorrow morning. If she knew for sure who it was, and had proof they had no rights, Sheriff Andrews would have no choice but to deal with them. He had made it clear he was in no hurry to investigate on her behalf, so it was up to her to take care of this.

"Oh my goodness," Cassia said, "that would be great. I really don't want to go back to the mansion tonight alone. What if they know it was me and come after me there?"

"You can stay with me, or I'll go back with you. We'll think of something. It's just for one night," Genevieve said.

"So, how do we do this?" Cassia asked.

"The best way is to go out to Roger's place and ask him. If this place wasn't going to be so packed tonight, he could come here, but there'll be too many people around," Genevieve said.

"What about your rush?"

"I have an idea for that," Genevieve said. "When you're done eating, come over here and help me roll up these napkins."

———

Two hours later, Genevieve and Cassia had prepared the diner completely for the Friday night fish fry. Genevieve had bribed Bridget, the hostess and backup waitress, into taking her Friday night shift if Genevieve would cover for her at the Apple Festival on Saturday.

"I'm going to have to hire you so I don't get in trouble with the state labor board," Trent called from the back.

"Fine with me," Cassia called back. "I need a job."

Genevieve shook her head at Cassia. "Never tell them you need a job. Say you'll think about it."

"I mean, I'll think about it," Cassia called.

Trent laughed in the back. "Genevieve, stop being a bad influence."

"Good, you mean good influence," Genevieve said.

"Whatever, have a good night off while we're working our fingers off in the kitchen," he said.

"Will do," Genevieve said. "We're leaving as soon as Bridget shows up."

Genevieve went back to the bathroom to change into a gray sweater and black jeans. "Nothing incognito about running around in this stylish blue dress." Cassia had to laugh. Genevieve could pull it off. She, on the other hand, would probably look like a sack of potatoes if she had to wear something like that blue retro number. Something to negotiate with Trent if she ever got so far as to get a job there.

Bridget arrived moments later, a fiftyish woman with light brown hair and an enormous smile.

"You must be Cassia. Nice to meet you. You wouldn't believe it, but this is going to be relaxing compared to spending the evening taking care of the grandkids. Their mom wasn't all that happy about my working tonight, but when she heard I'll take them to the Apple festival tomorrow, that made it all okay," Bridget said to Cassia in one breath.

Cassia took a step back. "Nice to meet you, too."

Genevieve pulled Cassia's arm. "Come on." She turned to Bridget. "Thanks so much."

They escaped out the back door, avoiding the crowd out front waiting for Trent to unlock the door.

Once they exited the alley to cool late afternoon air on Main Street, Genevieve breathed a sigh of relief. "Ah, a beautiful Friday night for adventure."

Adventure? Weren't they just going to get the name of that company? The knot in Cassia's chest started to tighten again.

They walked halfway down the block when Cassia remembered. "Wait, my bike." She motioned back to the diner.

"Go grab it," Genevieve said. "I'm sure we can get it in the backseat or something."

Cassia ran back and unlocked the bike locked one store front down from the diner. She was glad they were leaving before the crowd got in. People filled the sidewalk and spilled onto the street. She put the U-lock back in its bracket and walked the bike down to Genevieve. She didn't notice the two men in the crowd staring after her.

CHAPTER 22

They reached Genevieve's blue Honda parked off on a side street, away from the meters.

Genevieve unlocked the doors and rearranged stuff in the backseat. Most of the groceries were gone, but a small stockpile of bags rested on the floor behind the driver's seat. Genevieve peeked in one of the bags. "We're all stocked. Ready to go meet the man."

They managed to get Cassia's bike shoved into the backseat by removing the front wheel.

Cassia climbed into the passenger seat. Genevieve started the car and they pulled away.

"So, do we have to go far?" Cassia asked.

"Not too bad," Genevieve said. "Not nearly as far as your place."

A few minutes later they arrived at a two-story yellow house, with wide wooden slats for siding and a front flower garden full of mechanical fans and gizmos that spun with the light breeze. Two garden gnomes guarded the front step leading up to the wide wooden porch.

"He makes garden knickknacks in his garage when he

doesn't have repair work," Genevieve said as they exited the car. Genevieve opened the back door, and pulled out a few tins of sardines and a carton of malted candy, and shut the door again.

They approached the house. Cassia paused to examine one of the spinning yard gizmos. It was not a simple fan blade on a stick, as she'd at first thought. Instead, it had complex gears spinning, and a small platform where tiny little metal animals danced as the blade spun. It reminded her of an old-fashioned clock tower she'd seen in a picture book of Prague.

"He makes these?" Cassia asked Genevieve.

"Yep."

"He should sell them."

"We all tell him," Genevieve said. "He says that would take all the fun out of it. But if you're nice, and he likes you, he'll give you one for free. Pay attention to whose yard has one in town."

Cassia pursed her lips as she stared at all the gizmos. Checking the other yards in the block, most had one or two in their own grass. "Is it a bad sign I've not seen anything like this at the mansion?"

"Well, it's not a great sign," Genevieve said. "Maybe they had someone else come and do the maintenance."

That was possible. Sarah did seem to have an aversion to town. Or maybe getting a certain maintenance company had been one of Aunt Mildred's rules. If she was anything like the will she'd written, she probably had a ton of them.

Or maybe they'd just skipped all maintenance, judging by the outside of the mansion.

Genevieve knocked on the door, then pressed a large ornate button where a doorbell should be. Chimes inside the house rang musically, drifting down to them from an open window on the second floor.

Cassia looked up at the window just in time to see Roger

lift the sash and lean out. He was not wearing his straw hat, and his long, wild, white hair seemed to go in every direction. He looked far too young to have white hair.

"Genny, good to see you," he said, smiling down at them. He nodded at Cassia.

"We brought treats," Genevieve said.

"Wonderful," he said. "How about ice tea in the backyard?"

"Perfect," Genevieve said.

"Go around," he said. "The garden gate's open. I'll meet you back there."

Brilliant flowers filled the back garden, from purple blooms climbing trellises along the back wall to the tiny deep red flowers in the groundcover nearest the grass. Taller versions of the metal garden sculptures filled the backyard, some with their own miniature wooden roofs to protect them from the rain. Muted wind chimes hung off the nearest edge of the garage, bringing their own music to the small space of flowers.

Cassia and Genevieve sat at the hand carved chairs and table set in the center of the garden. The scale was a little off. Cassia's feet could not quite reach the ground when sitting in her chair. Neither could Genevieve's. It gave Cassia the distinct sense of being six years old again.

A few minutes later, Roger emerged, his straw hat back on, and carrying a large tray with a pitcher of iced tea, glasses with ice, and a tray of lemon cookies. He set the tray down in the middle of the table and poured iced tea for everyone. "I hope a little sweet is okay."

Cassia took the offered tea and took a sip. It was sweet and lemony and cool. There was something about this town. Everyone here seemed to be able to cook better than she could.

"Thanks for the cookies," Genevieve said. She pushed over the tins of sardines and the candy to Roger.

"Of course. I know not everyone has my taste in treats," he

said with a wink to Genevieve. He put the sardines in the front pocket of his flannel shirt and set the carton of candy down next to his chair.

They all three sat in silence for a moment.

"Oh, I'm sorry," Genevieve said. "Roger, this is Cassia. Cassia, this is Roger."

Roger nodded at Cassia. "From the mansion, right?"

"Yes," Cassia said.

"Sorry about the trouble you had out there," he said.

"Yes, me too," Cassia said, remembering that Roger had been one of the people to come and take the body of Brody Johnson away.

"Any word on what happened to that young man?" Roger asked.

"No, not yet. Did you know him?" Cassia asked. Maybe Roger knew more people than Genevieve had.

"No… not really. I'd seen him around before a few times. He was related to that old housekeeper," Roger said.

Cassia sat up. "You worked at the mansion?"

Roger shook his head. "Well, once or twice, back in the day. I barely recognized that boy now. He was so much younger when I'd seen him before. They had some change in management or something and stopped calling for my help."

"You know why he would've been out there?" Cassia asked. She ignored Genevieve's stare.

"That I do not," Roger said. "I do know that old lady gave him an envelope of money once. I wasn't supposed to see that, but I was working on the back shed and I guess she forgot I was there."

"Old lady? The housekeeper or…" For some reason, Cassia couldn't bring herself to say Aunt Mildred. How was she was addressed by the townspeople? Mrs. Mildred Mandress?

"The housekeeper, Mrs. Johnson, but I'll wager she got that

money from Mrs. Mandress." Roger answered better than Cassia could have hoped for.

Cassia nodded, then grabbed a cookie and nibbled on it while she thought about that answer. If Brody Johnson was used to getting money from coming to visit the mansion, then that would be one reason to come by. But then, how did he end up on the roof of the observatory? And how could he not know that Mildred Mandress was dead, and his grandmother Rose Johnson had been dead for some time before that?

"Actually, that's not why we're here, or at least that's not the only reason," Genevieve said.

"What? You mean you're not here to just be social with me?" Roger said, a teasing glint in his eye as he clutched his heart and mimed being mortally wounded.

"Well, besides that, of course. Cassia saw some people on the land out back and was wondering if you knew who they might be based on the logo on their trucks. I figured if anyone knew all the companies around here, it would be you. You probably fixed all those trucks ten times over."

"More than likely," Roger said.

Cassia pulled out her phone and opened it to the pictures. She zoomed in on a still frame from the video that had the best image of the logo on it and handed the phone over to Roger.

He took the phone and peered at the image. "Oh yeah, I know that company. Might not help you much, though."

"Why?" Cassia and Genevieve asked in unison.

"It's a rental outfit. You have to call and ask them or take a closer look. That could be just about anyone using those trucks."

Cassia exhaled and put her head in her hands.

"If I do remember correctly though," Roger said, "they rent by the week. Monday morning to Monday morning. If you saw those trucks recently, whoever has them now probably had them then."

"Do they rent the garage, too?" Genevieve asked. Cassia looked at her questioningly. "I mean, they sound like big trucks. Maybe they don't always have them on the worksite. It might be one place to look."

"That I don't know," Roger said. "They are some monster big trucks." He looked off with a blissful expression.

———

Cassia and Genevieve walked back to the car, each carrying a small paper sack. The sun was setting and long shafts of orange-gold light hit the houses around them. Cassia felt sluggish and ready for bed, but she didn't want to go back to the mansion.

Genevieve unlocked the car and they both got in.

"That was nice of him, to make us sandwiches," Cassia said. Roger had insisted on giving them food to go, tuna fish, of course, but the sandwiches also had celery, lettuce and tomato from his garden.

"He's a nice guy, I told you," Genevieve said. She tucked her bag behind her seat and pulled out a piece of paper from her jacket pocket. "You know, we could drive by this place and see if there's any cars parked from the people who rented them?"

"How would that help us?" Cassia asked. "It's not like we can look up license plates or anything to see where they live or their names."

"We could follow them home," Genevieve said. "Besides, it's a small-town sort of deal. Maybe I'll recognize them from the diner."

Cassia sincerely hoped that the people frequenting the diner were not the sort to shoot strangers in the woods.

"Or I could take you back to the mansion," Genevieve said, side-eyeing Cassia.

"You promised! Unless you're coming back there to stay with me, no," Cassia said.

"Baby."

"Yes."

Cassia pulled out her own phone. It only had twenty percent charge left. "Do you have a charger I can use?" she asked Genevieve.

"I might have some," Genevieve said. She pushed Cassia's knees out of the way and pulled out a battery pack and charging cable from the glove box. She offered it to Cassia.

Cassia stared at her.

"What?" Genevieve asked, offering the pack again. "My cigarette lighter doesn't work. They broke it when they tried to fix the dash light. Something about old plastic. It's all right, I'm sharing. With my exciting life of going back and forth to the diner, I don't usually worry about my phone charge."

Cassia took the battery pack and cable and hooked it up to her phone.

"Okay, now I've given you some juice, let's go spy on these guys," Genevieve said.

"You are not going to give this a rest, are you?" Cassia asked.

"Nope."

It would be nice to know who these guys were. If they had information ready when Nate called in the morning, they could go right to the sheriff and insist he do something about it. She had video evidence.

That is, if they didn't have rights and they were poaching in her woods. If they did have rights, and they shot her anyway, then they were just nuts, and she was nuts for even thinking about going anywhere near them.

"Look, we'll just drive by. There's no way they'll think to be looking for my old car. Everyone in town knows you were pulling up in that massive twelve-foot white truck."

"Was. That truck is gone."

"Do you think those guys know that?"

Probably not, Cassia admitted.

"Come on," Genevieve said, coaxing Cassia. "Don't you want those guys to pay for shooting at you? For stealing your stuff? For ruining your woods that you don't even own yet?"

Yeah, Cassia really kind of did want that. It was always possible that Nate would call tomorrow and say that this company had the rights to her woods, but somehow she didn't believe that. They would have just come over and talked to her instead of pulling out the firearms, because as Deputy Chester said, it was not hunting season.

Against her better judgment, Cassia turned to Genevieve and said, "All right, let's go find these guys."

CHAPTER 23

Cassia and Genevieve rolled over the two-lane highway in Genevieve's old Honda, the tires humming on the smooth road. Thick clouds overhead prevented the moon or stars from illuminating the road, leaving the pine trees that lined both sides of the road as black hulking shadows that hemmed them in.

The air smelled of rain, even more than it had outside the diner. The weather rolled by fast in the Midwest, much faster than she'd seen in Southern California where the sunshine would stay for days and days. Here, storms flew by in minutes, with more storms lined up behind to come sweeping in on their own time.

Cassia rolled down the window a crack. A sharp breeze came in with the bite of coldness. Cassia shivered and she rolled up the window. She'd left her jacket in the woods and her hoodie was not enough against the slight dampness in the air. She pulled up her hood and rubbed her arms to warm them.

Genevieve glanced over at Cassia's shivering and turned up the heat. She blasted the vent at Cassia. Genevieve had programmed the destination into her phone and put it in a holder clip that attached to the heat vent. Now, Cassia watched their progress on the tiny map on the cell phone screen with dread and fascination as she held up her hands to the heat vents to absorb as much warmth as possible.

"This seems pretty far away," Cassia said.

"It's a bit. Guess not too many places rent that sort of big logging equipment."

"How did Roger know of them?"

Genevieve gave a small laugh. "I told you, he's the best in three counties."

"You don't have much juice either," Cassia said, indicating Genevieve's phone. "What if we get in trouble and need to make a call?"

"We better not get in trouble then," Genevieve said.

Cassia glared at her. Cassia liked to plan ahead. This was not planning ahead.

In the low moonlight, Genevieve's spiky hair really did look like an exotic manga hairdo. All that was missing was the dramatic sword and strange outfit to make the look complete.

Genevieve ignored Cassia's glare so Cassia looked at the road ahead. The car's headlights barely lit it up, the orange lines seeming to disappear just a few feet in front of the car.

"Are your lights on?" Cassia asked.

"Yeah, but they're probably dirty and old. They're not very bright."

That could describe this mission, Cassia thought. What had seemed so easy an hour ago in the safety of early evening in a small town now seemed much more intimidating on a dark road in the middle of nowhere.

"Maybe we should just go back," Cassia said.

"Maybe," Genevieve said.

The car kept going straight.

The truck rental company was three towns over, at the edge of the tiny town. Cassia and Genevieve's car emerged from the deep darkness of the road through the woods into the light spilling out from the fast food strip and mega-grocery store ahead that also huddled on this side of the town. A chain-link fence surrounded the tall metal building of the rental company that could have doubled as an airline hanger, the logo from the truck clearly visible on the side of the building.

The rental company building was the closest one to the woods on the left side of the road. A dark and decrepit strip mall faced it across the street.

"That's our place," Genevieve said, turning off the navigation on her phone to save the battery.

They pulled closer, taking advantage of the lower speed limit in town to stare at the rental company. The gate on the fence around the building stood open to the road. Cassia checked her phone. Despite feeling like the middle of the night, it was only nine p.m.

As they rolled by, Cassia craned her neck to stare inside. She saw one tall orange truck with a large claw, and another truck with the metal front assembly used to push over trees. This was definitely the type of equipment she'd seen earlier that day. It might be the very same equipment.

Genevieve let the car go past the rental company, then pulled into the parking lot of the grocery store. "Did you see anybody?"

"No. Just the equipment. It looks like the right stuff." Cassia said. She twisted in her seat to stare back at the rental company, but they were too far away.

Genevieve neatly rolled the car between two other parked cars in a row close to the grocery store.

"We go back and take a look," Genevieve said.

"We could, I suppose, but if we drive too many times back and forth they'll notice." There were no shrubs around the fence, or any trees on the property. Everything here felt oddly open and exposed after the last hour they spent driving through the woods.

"True. Too bad we can't just walk by, but there's nothing on the other side to walk to. We'd be so obvious," Genevieve said. She pulled out her sandwich from behind her seat and unwrapped it, and took a bite. The smell of tuna fish and sandwich spread filled the car. That was enough for Cassia to grab her own sandwich. They sat and ate and thought about what they should do.

"Too bad we don't have a dog," Cassia said.

Genevieve raised one eyebrow and looked at Cassia.

"It's a good excuse for a walk. We could just say we need to walk our dog." Cassia motioned walking about in the direction of the rental company.

"Great. Let me just see if I can borrow a dog from someone here at the store," Genevieve said. She leaned in and opened the glove box and pulled out a couple of napkins and gave Cassia one.

"It was just an idea," Cassia said.

Genevieve grunted and waved away any more ideas from Cassia.

"Fine. Be that way. I'm gonna go get a drink while we're thinking about this," Cassia said.

Cassia pulled her wallet from her messenger bag and opened the door and got out. She walked to the bright lights of the mega-grocery store. Genevieve didn't move from the driver's seat.

A few moments later, Cassia ran back to the car, opened the door and got back in. She shut the door as quietly as she could. She could feel it not quite latch.

"Not a good idea, not a good idea, not a good idea," Cassia

muttered under her breath. "Look down," she hissed to Genevieve.

Startled, Genevieve stopped chewing, but did as she was told and looked down to her lap. Cassia did the same, shaking her head to let her hair fall in front of her eyes. Two men walked by one aisle ahead of them, passing in front of Genevieve's car. Cassia strained to hear their footsteps as they walked past. Their pace hadn't seemed to waver. Hopefully, they hadn't seen her, or better yet, didn't even know who she was.

Cassia slowly looked up through her hair hanging in front of her face. The men were walking across the parking lot toward the rental building carrying several grocery bags. One of the men was huge, dwarfing the second man.

He also wore a black and red check jacket and matching hat.

Cassia's heart raced and her skin felt clammy. She recognized that man from the convenience store. He was the one yelling at Sarah, talking about some deal they had. Now she regretted not asking Sarah directly about him and what her connection was with him.

His being here could just be a coincidence, but that man was scary on a good day.

Genevieve looked up and followed Cassia's gaze. "Who's that?"

"That's the guy I told you about yelling at Sarah." Cassia turned in her seat to watch the men as they turned at the bottom of the parking lot and walked along the edge of the road toward the rental building.

"He's huge," Genevieve said.

Cassia glared at her. "I told you."

Genevieve shrugged. "I'm sorry. They are all huge. Okay, they're not that huge, but you have to admit they all wear flannel."

Cassia waved her away.

They turned back to watch the men as they picked their way along the road, then turned in the driveway to the rental agency and walked into the huge open garage door of the large building.

———

Cassia and Genevieve sat in the front seat, drinking waters Genevieve had dug out from underneath the passenger seat. The cars in the parking lot of the mega-grocery store had thinned, leaving Cassia feeling more exposed.

"Okay, one, he knows Sarah, which means he probably knows about the mansion, also means he probably has something to do with it," Cassia said, trying to get her thoughts organized by listing out the facts. "Two, there is lumber work happening on the mansion grounds, and apparently he either rents out or is renting some lumber equipment."

"Those are some tightly related facts," Genevieve said.

"Yes."

"But no smoking gun."

Cassia stared at Genevieve.

"Isn't that a saying? Of course, he could have an actual smoking gun if he was the one that shot you today…" Genevieve said, trying to make a joke.

"Not. Funny." Cassia still didn't feel right from what happened that morning. She shook just thinking about it.

"Right. Sorry. We could just go tell Sheriff Andrews about the guy," said Genevieve. "I mean, Sarah knows who he is."

"But would she admit that?" Cassia asked. "What if she just denied it?"

"Would she?"

Cassia threw up her hands. "I have no idea. One minute

the woman is warm and friendly, and the next she is pricklier than a pear."

"A what?"

"Nevermind. I'm sure it's a saying in some universe."

Genevieve took another sip of her water. "What are we gonna do in this universe? I gotta work in the morning. Plus, they might lock the gate up. We should've taken pictures of them when we had a chance."

Genevieve was right. They could have filmed the two men walking into the rental company. It wasn't a sure bet, but it would definitely have linked them to some sort of logging activity. Actually, it would have been pretty good, Cassia realized. They had photos of that company's logo on trucks in her woods. A video of the men walking into the same rental company on the same day was a strong link.

Dang it. That would've been the easiest. Take a video and go home.

"What kind of zoom do you have on your camera?" Genevieve asked, while holding her own phone and trying to film the rental agency from their spot. It looked like one blurry mass in the low light.

"Probably not any better than yours," Cassia said.

"We could park closer."

Cassia twisted in her seat and eyed the parking lot closest to the rental building. It was a vast open space with the only vehicle in it an old pickup truck about two thirds of the way to the rental building. "Is that truck bigger than your car?"

"We shall see," Genevieve said, twisting the key in the ignition and bringing the engine to life.

"I... I was just asking," Cassia said quietly, gripping the door handle tightly even though Genevieve drove slowly through the lot. She hunched down and looked away from the building, keeping a curtain of her hair between her face and the large open bay of the rental building's garage door.

Glancing at Genevieve, she pulled down the driver's side sun visor and tried to hide Genevieve's face.

Genevieve pulled up next to the truck. Her car neatly fitting behind it.

"Great, now we can't see them at all," Cassia said. Her relief at being out of the sight lines of the building fighting with the dread that the men inside could sneak up on them now unseen.

"We can see them if we get out of the car," Genevieve said patiently.

That involved getting out of the car around people who might be carrying guns and could be dangerous. Not that cars were much protection against guns. Cassia knew they weren't. She'd seen a documentary. Everyone thought they were good, though, because of all the TV shows that used that.

Suddenly, Cassia wished she was at home watching a TV show.

Adventure was overrated.

There was only one way to get this over with.

"Okay," Cassia said, turning to Genevieve. "Do you have any spare clothes in this car? Like a winter coat or big shirt?"

"I might have something." Genevieve turned in her seat and pulled at the bags wedged behind the bike in the backseat.

———

Twenty minutes later, Genevieve and Cassia wore some very wrinkled oversized items from Genevieve's emergency stash for car accidents and blizzards. Being that they were for emergency use only, she'd picked them up at the local thrift store and hadn't cared much what they looked like, which meant Cassia and Genevieve now had on men's oversized flannel shirts in hideous shades of brown, orange, and black, along with a couple of black bucket hats, and even an enormous pair of snow pants Cassia had grabbed for herself.

Cassia struggled to pull the clothes over what she was already wearing while in the passenger seat with the seat pushed back. Genevieve, a few inches taller than Cassia, and dealing with the steering wheel, gave up and opened the door and pulled on her set of disguise clothing outside. Until this week, Genevieve had nothing to do with the mansion, so anyone seeing her wouldn't guess that she was spying because of logging on the mansion grounds.

When Cassia got the snow pants on, and buttoned up the brown and black flannel, she pulled up her hood, and pulled the bucket hat down over it. It was a tight fit, but she was able to get the hat low enough to hide most of her face.

"How do I look?" she asked Genevieve.

Genevieve bent over and looked in the open car door. "Ridiculous."

"But can you tell if I'm a girl?"

"I can't tell if you're human."

Good enough.

The plan was they would act like two drunk old bums staggering around the parking lot and maybe walking toward the street and the rental agency. It was all intended to look like an accident. Genevieve had found an old empty fifth of scotch on the edge of the parking lot and had come up with the idea. It was better than Cassia's original idea of putting on a disguise and walking past as quickly as possible.

As long as they were not too entertaining as bums, everyone should ignore them.

CHAPTER 24

Cassia and Genevieve ambled on the edge of the parking lot, slowly heading toward the grass beyond, and then to the street that ran by the rental company.

Despite the chill in the air, bugs swarmed around the tall lights in the mega-grocery store parking lot, flying in and out of the mist and giving a flickering look to the asphalt below. Katydids sang in the tall grass, punctuated by the occasional bell like "ting" from overhead as a large moth smashed into the light above.

Genevieve made a show swinging the liquor bottle, now half filled with cola and water mixed to look like whiskey. Cassia fumbled with her phone. The oversized sleeves on her shirt made it easy to hide it, but also made it difficult to film. She tried to aim the phone's camera lens out between the slit in the back of the sleeve where it normally buttoned shut.

Behind them, the parking lot was mostly empty. Cassia wanted to hurry before the grocery store shut for the night and the rest of the cars left. With any luck, the pickup truck belonged to an employee who was staying at least until close, or better yet all night for stocking. If that truck pulled away, it would leave Genevieve's car in plain sight of the rental place.

"See anybody?" Cassia whispered.

Genevieve swung around drunkenly, letting her eyes pass over the rental building. "No. Lights still on. Door still open. Isn't it late for that?"

"Yes."

"Maybe they're waiting for someone," Genevieve said, mumbling her words, but still louder than Cassia was comfortable with. It took all of Cassia's willpower to not turn and look back at the grocery store for the fifth or sixth time. Her back tingled with the effort. She was sure someone was staring at them.

"Let's hurry," Cassia said, trying to pull off a quicker drunken walk.

The minutes ticked by agonizingly slow as they made their way to the front of the drive of the rental place. A small office door was set in the far corner of the building, on the side away from the grocery store. Lights were on in the office, but the blinds were pulled shut, making it impossible to see if anyone was inside.

Next to the office door, the massive two-story garage door stood open. Lights blazed within the cavernous space and spilled out the large opening to the driveway and the street beyond. Inside the garage, large orange trucks sat parked along the walls, with open space in the middle for several more machines.

Glancing down at her hand, Cassia pulled back her sleeve to check the position of her phone. The inside of the rental building wobbled on the screen as she walked, showing she'd aimed in the right direction.

When they stood near the center of the driveway, Genevieve grabbed Cassia's sleeve and pulled her to a stop, her other arm holding up the liquor bottle and pretending to drink from it. Cassia used that moment to turn off the video recording and take pictures of the building and the equipment inside. A few of the trucks were parked sideways inside the building, leaving the logo showing. Hopefully her phone's resolution was enough to show it.

"Okay. I think we've got it," Cassia whispered. She slipped the phone in the pocket of the snow pants.

At that moment, bright truck headlights appeared at the turn of the road coming out of the forest. The roar of a diesel engine echoed in the air around them.

"That's probably coming for this garage," Genevieve whispered. They turned to hustle back to the grocery store, only to see three men coming through the parking lot toward them, talking among themselves and carrying grocery bags. The men had not seen them yet. Cassia's heart stopped when she saw how two of them were dressed. They had on the same black and red check jackets and hats that the mountain of a man she had recognized had wore. They must be related somehow.

Genevieve and Cassia turned once again, stuck between the oncoming truck from one direction and the men in the other direction. If they ran across the road to the strip mall the truck would see them for sure.

They looked at each other and at the open maw of the rental company's garage then ran for it.

———

Cassia and Genevieve huddled on the running board of one of the trucks lined against the far wall. It was one of those with a gigantic crane and claw at the end. It smelled like dirt and earth, having been freshly used. Clumps of sod still clung in the tines of the claw.

No one had come out of the rightmost small door inside the garage that must lead to the inner office when they'd snuck in. They'd run to the opening of the garage door, peered inside, and having seen no one, heel toed it as quietly and quickly as they could to the back of the garage and then around the truck to hide behind it.

Genevieve opened her mouth and Cassia held up a finger to silence her.

A few seconds later, the three men rounded the corner and entered the garage, their voices filling it.

"I'm telling you, double overtime isn't even enough," one man said. "It's Friday freaking night and here we are."

"He bought us snacks," another voice said.

"Snacks? I should be on a date with Rochelle. I don't want no freaking snacks. At least not that kind, if you know what I mean," the first voice said.

"No," the second voice said, clearly not knowing what the first man meant.

A third voice said, "Ah, jeez," which was quickly followed up with the sound of a hand smacking the back of someone's head.

"Ouch," said the second voice.

The door inside the garage that led to the office opened and then fell shut again with a slam. The men's voices were gone.

Cassia bent down to see if she could look underneath the vehicle but couldn't get down low enough without losing her balance. She scooted forward on the running board as silently as she could, then reached out one foot and put it down behind the wheel so that someone on the other side of the vehicle would not see her standing on the ground. Wiggling forward, she got both feet on the ground, then leaned around the front end of the vehicle. No one was in the garage.

Slowly, she circled the front end of the truck and checked the space. She was about to step around to the other side when the handle of the inner door banged. Scrambling, she ran back around to the back of the truck.

Just as she got both feet back up on the running board, headlights turned the corner on the driveway outside and the truck they'd seen in the distance pulled in. It was larger than the other trucks and filled most of the space in the center. Its headlights shone on the wall behind Cassia and Genevieve. Diesel exhaust filled the space. Cassia choked back a cough.

Finally, the engine cut out. Cassia's lungs burned.

The truck's cab door opened. Someone got out, their heavy boots thumping on the concrete floor, and slammed the door shut again before walking away. Seconds later, the massive garage door running on tracks along the ceiling jerked to life and started sliding forward and down. The noise echoed around the tin and concrete garage like a jet engine. The garage door landed on the concrete with a heavy bang.

A minute later, the lights went out, and the door to the inner office slammed shut.

Genevieve and Cassia waited in the darkness. Cassia reached out a hand to make sure Genevieve was next to her. The garage had no windows, and without the lights, it was pitch-black.

"Now what?" Genevieve whispered.

———

Cassia's heart thudded in her ears. She couldn't see anything. The complete blackness of the garage of the rental business enveloped everything. Beside her, Genevieve breathed heavily.

"Well, what should we do?" Genevieve whispered in a hoarse voice.

"Wait. Let's be quiet and wait for a few minutes. They might come right back," Cassia said.

They waited. The acrid smell of the diesel exhaust from

the newly parked truck mixed with the smells of dirt and rotting organic matter and oil from the other trucks. Somewhere, something dripped off one of the machines, lending an ominous *tick tick tick* to the background.

A muffled, howling laugh came from the inner office door.

"They're still there," Cassia whispered.

"I heard," Genevieve whispered back. She didn't sound good, the hoarseness in her voice intensifying.

"You okay?" Cassia said.

"Yeah, fine. I just want out of here."

Cassia did too. Those guys couldn't stay here all night.

They breathed in and waited in the cavernous garage. Another burst of laughter came.

Genevieve shifted uneasily on her side of the runner board. She felt for the ground with one foot and got off the truck and then sat down on the running board.

"What if they come back?" Cassia asked.

"I'll lift my feet," Genevieve said.

As the tedium of the minutes wore on, Cassia's panicky fear slowly turned to boredom.

"If we get outside, we could go around the office window and spy in, maybe take a photo," she suggested.

Genevieve grunted. "If we get outside, we could go to my car and go home."

"Or both," Cassia suggested.

"Daring."

"I want this over as much as you do," Cassia said defensively. "Wasn't it your idea to come out here to begin with?"

Silence met this. Finally, Genevieve said. "True that. We've got some stuff to finish."

Cassia felt around in the voluminous pockets of her snow pants until she found her cell phone. She flicked it on. Five percent power. "Wait here."

"What?" Genevieve asked, but it was too late.

Cassia shuffled around the front of the truck they were hiding behind and scooted along the outer wall, keeping behind the vehicles parked along there. She turned on her phone's flashlight and shone ahead, then turned it off and ran the short distance she knew was clear. She repeated the process until she was by the main garage door.

The sound of the men was louder there. Individual voices sounded behind the door, not quite loud enough to make out the words, punctuated by laughter and the occasional "ouch".

Hurrying, Cassia ran her flashlight over the wall by the garage door until she found the control pad. Her heart sank. The square pad surrounded a circle with a slit in it for a key, and not a button, as Cassia had been hoping. If there had been a button, all they would have had to do was wait for the men to leave and then push the button and leave themselves.

She checked the other side of the garage door. There were no other controls. A flutter of panic started in her heart again. They didn't have a key.

She quickly retraced her steps back to the truck at the rear of the garage, but when she flashed her cell phone light at the far side of the truck, Genevieve was gone. Cassia quickly shut the light off again. "Genevieve," she whispered in a panic.

"Over here," Genevieve called quietly from the far wall of the garage, the one that led up toward the office. "I saw a side door." A few moments later, a quiet clicking rang out. "Dang it," Genevieve said.

"Shhh," Cassia said as loud as she dared.

Genevieve returned, flashing her own cell phone occasionally as Cassia had.

"There's a side door over there, but it locks with a key." Genevieve said.

"How fast a runner are you?" Cassia asked.

"Not that fast."

They sat in silence in the darkness for a moment.

"How are you doing for power?" Genevieve asked.

Cassia checked her phone. "Three percent. You?"

"Four percent. We could call for help unlocking the door when they leave, but my phone's not going to make it unless they go soon."

As if reading her mind, the door to the inner office opened and five men exited into the garage space. One of them flicked on the lights, and their voices boomed and echoed around the hard surfaces of the room.

"Sure you don't want to come with us? Rochelle said there was extra company," a voice said.

"No, not tonight. I got some work I've got to take care of," a familiar voice said. Cassia recognized it as the voice of the man at the gas station. The one who had yelled at Sarah. Her stomach curdled. She looked over at Genevieve who was focused on balancing precariously on the running board, hugging her legs in so they wouldn't show beneath the truck.

"Your loss," the first man said. "Let me just get my stuff and we're outta here. Tomorrow then."

"Tomorrow," gas station man said. A series of truck doors opened and shut as lunch pails and jackets were pulled from the cabs. The inner door opened, and the men filed out, followed by a slam.

The men had left the lights on.

Cassia and Genevieve looked at each other and waited.

The only noise in the garage was the *tick tick tick* from the dripping truck.

Cassia expected to hear another door in the distance as the men left the building and walked off. What actually she heard next was the gas station man's voice speaking close by in the garage. "Hello, ladies."

CHAPTER 25

Cassia gasped. She felt momentarily faint. White showed around Genevieve's eyes as she stared back at Cassia.

The harsh overhead lighting illuminated every corner of the garage, bouncing off the orange trucks and the white washed walls and the concrete floor. There was no place to hide in the cavernous space except behind the trucks.

"Aren't you going to say hi?" the man asked. "That's not very polite." He walked slowly, his heavy work boots thudding on the concrete floor.

Cassia grasped the side of the truck to keep from falling off the running board. She scanned the nearby walls looking for anything that could be used as a weapon: a crowbar, a jack, anything that could be thrown, but the back wall was bare. All the shelving and equipment was on the side wall that ran toward the front office. There was no easy way to reach it without the man seeing them.

"I'm waiting," the man said. "I know you're here. I saw it on the security cameras. And you thought you were so sneaky coming into the garage. I couldn't believe how easy you've made my day by coming to me."

Cassia looked at Genevieve in a panic. Genevieve shook her head. She didn't know what to do either.

"You know, I can be a nice person, but I won't be nice if you continue to make me wait."

Cassia's hands shook as she held onto the truck. She called out, her voice unsteady. "If we're on the security camera, then other people will know we're here too."

The man chuckled. "Oh, no no no. They won't. Now you're insulting my intelligence. While my perennially hungry workers were off getting munchies, I erased the security camera footage, then helped it have a little accident with my foot. It's not going now. Sorry, girls. But you know, that sort of equipment is always breaking. No one will think a thing of it."

He stopped pacing.

Tick tick tick went the drip.

"You can just open the door and let us go," Cassia called. "We didn't take anything. We're just curious about big trucks and stuff."

"Oh you say that, but I saw you this morning spying on my crew." he said, drawing out the words lazily. "You're too curious about my business, and that does not make me happy." He resumed his pacing. Slowly, he made his way closer to the rear of the truck they were hiding behind. Genevieve quietly put her feet on the ground and stood crouched, ready to run.

"I was just going for a walk in the woods," Cassia said. "There's nothing wrong with that."

"You see, some folks might see it that way, but I don't," he said. "The way I see it, is those are my woods, and you had no business back there. I don't like people spying on me."

Genevieve mouthed "he's nuts" at Cassia. Cassia nodded.

"Is that why you shot at me?" Cassia asked.

"My gun might have accidentally gone off," he said. He continued coming closer to the rear of the truck. Cassia and

Genevieve slowly crept around to the front, keeping the vehicle between them.

"You're shy, I guess. That's okay," he said. He did not seem pleased.

"You can keep your woods," Cassia said in a rush. "I don't care. I didn't know. I'm new here. All you have to do is tell me and they're all yours."

He laughed again. "As if it was that easy." Suddenly, he kicked the rear end of the truck they were hiding behind. The crunch of the bumper echoed against the walls.

Cassia and Genevieve jumped back.

"No," he said, an edge of anger in his voice. "I don't trust you folk. Always changing your mind. It's never good enough. We'll come to one agreement, and then you'll change your mind and say the deal's off or ask for more money or just be a pain in my side. I know you."

Cassia wondered who he was talking about. He seemed to be having a conversation with someone else—a someone else he really didn't like.

"No, I'm different," Cassia said. "I keep my word. Just open the door and let us go."

He didn't reply. He resumed walking, coming around the back of the truck. Cassia and Genevieve scooted around to the other side, then ran to another vehicle and hid behind it. Cassia's snow pants dragged on the concrete. She grabbed at the loose material and pulled them up, but they'd already made a lot of sound.

"I'm not going to hit you," he said. "You can stop running."

"That's okay," Cassia said. "Like you said, we're shy." She wanted to keep him talking. The longer they talked, the better chance she and Genevieve would have of finding something to use as a weapon. He pinned them on the side of the garage away from the shelving. If they could just get over there, they'd have a chance of getting something to use to protect themselves.

"Who was the terrible person who broke their word to you?" Cassia asked, trying to sound sympathetic.

"Who hasn't?" he said.

Genevieve shook her head at that, not impressed. She was looking at something on her phone. Cassia ignored her and concentrated on keeping the man distracted.

"Did Brody break his word?" Cassia asked. Genevieve looked up at her sharply.

"Who?" He sounded confused.

"The old housekeeper's son," Cassia said. "About my age."

"That twerp," he said. "Like I would ever listen to him for any reason. Always begging for money."

"So you didn't kill him?" Cassia asked.

The man laughed, genuinely amused. "I wouldn't even have to bother. The last time I saw that twerp, he was running across the roof, probably high as a kite."

"You saw him at the mansion?" Cassia asked.

Genevieve gave her a thumbs-up.

"Oh, yes. Babbling about Grandma Johnson leaving him a message. Sarah, curse her lying soul, took care of that."

"Sarah the housekeeper from the mansion?" Cassia asked.

"Housekeeper, ha! Is that what she calls herself these days?"

"That's what she told me. Was she lying?" Cassia asked.

"Enough talk," he said and stepped around the truck they were hiding behind, a gun held high.

Cassia and Genevieve screamed and ran. Genevieve dropped her phone. It exploded, sending parts skidding on the concrete.

He fired a shot after them as they scrambled between the trucks. It bounced off the truck they just left and ricocheted again off the wall, flying past Cassia's eye with a whine.

Cassia and Genevieve ran past the shelves of jacks, oil cans, and other truck equipment in their scramble to find another hiding spot. They quickly grabbed what they could as they went by. Cassia lucked out with a tire iron. Genevieve got an oil pan and a bottle of oil.

Twice he ran after them around the garage. Each time they managed to keep ahead and out of line of his gun. Cassia panted heavily, sweating in the ridiculous snow pants and flannel shirt. Her chest hurt trying to pull in air.

After the second time around, Genevieve turned and threw the oil pan back like a frisbee. It flew through the air and skidded on the concrete and under his feet just as he turned the corner. He put one foot on it and lost his balance as it slid out from underneath him.

He went down like a mountain, but managed to hold on to the gun.

Cassia and Genevieve waited behind a truck, trying to catch their breath.

"Office… door," Cassia whispered between pants. Genevieve nodded.

He groaned and slowly got to his feet. Holding the gun in their direction he limped toward the office door and locked it. "I heard you, my pretties, but too bad for you… now I'm mad."

Genevieve grabbed Cassia's hand and held it tight. They crouched and waited, ready to run no matter which way he came.

But instead of chasing after them, he limped toward the gigantic truck in the middle of the garage.

Opening the door, he climbed into the cab. He left the door open and his left hand held the gun out ready to shoot, while he started the engine with his right. The truck roared to life.

"He's crazy," Genevieve said under her breath. She squeezed Cassia's hand so tightly it hurts Cassia's knuckles.

He revved the engine several times.

The foul-smelling diesel fumes reached Cassia, making it even harder to breathe.

Stepping back out on the running board, he fiddled with the cab door, then slammed it shut, leaving the truck running.

He limped to the door to the inner office. "Have a nice *rest*, ladies" he said with a sickly emphasis on the word rest. A moment later, he was gone and the office door slammed shut behind him.

Cassia and Genevieve looked at each other.

"What's he doing?" Cassia asked, but she realized the answer just as she said it. The carbon monoxide from the diesel truck fumes would kill them if they didn't get out of there. She already felt ill from the smell.

They ran to the cab of the running truck. Genevieve climbed on the running board and tried to open the door while Cassia watched the office door with her crowbar at the ready.

"Locked," Genevieve hissed.

Cassia ran to the office door and tried it. It, too, was locked. She slammed the tire iron on the door handle. The handle flew off. She pushed at the door, but it didn't budge. She kicked it, pain reverberating up her leg when it didn't move.

He'd thrown a deadbolt on the other side. There was no way she could break down the metal door.

Coughing, Cassia ran back to Genevieve at the truck. "We have to get out of here," she said, her voice wheezing.

Genevieve shook her off, doing something with a card and some thin string wrapped around it.

"What are you doing? We have to break down a door!" Cassia said.

Genevieve coughed. "Trust me." She looked at Cassia's hand on her arm, trying to pull her away. "Stop grabbing me."

Cassia stepped back, confused. She ran the circuit of the

garage again, trying the doors one more time and smashing at anything she could with the tire iron. Nothing gave.

She went back to the truck. Genevieve had wedged the thread behind the seal of the driver's side door and pulled it down so that it ran in a line inside the cab from the top of the door to the side. A tiny loop hovered just over the handle lock.

Realizing her mistake, Cassia backed up and ran to the other side of the truck. She smashed the passenger side window with the tire iron. The window cracked but wouldn't break. She hit it again. The stuff was indestructible.

She tried the windshield with the same results.

"Got it!" Genevieve yelled. She yanked open the door as Cassia ran around the truck to her.

"No! Don't turn it off!" Cassia yelled. She shoved Genevieve into the truck and then climbed up after her, getting behind the driver's side. Grinding the gears in a horrible screeching, Cassia put the truck in reverse and slammed on the gas.

The truck ground backwards while making a horrible noise until Genevieve grabbed a lever and pushed the button to release it. The parking brakes let go and the truck jerked backwards and through the large garage door, ripping the door off its rails and dragging it outside in a spray of twisted metal and broken bolts as it shot out of the building, crossed the street, and crossed into the strip mall parking lot. It crashed into a hair salon, sending standup dryers and chairs everywhere.

CHAPTER 26

An alarm blasted in the dark beauty shop and red emergency lights flashed and reflected on the truck halfway in the shop through the shattered plate glass window. Somewhere in the back, water ran.

Inside the truck's cab, Cassia stirred. Her head hurt, along with her right shoulder. Nothing felt broken. Next to her, Genevieve moaned and slowly sat up.

"You're driving sucks," Genevieve said. She reached to open the passenger door.

"Don't," Cassia said. She pointed across the street to the rental building with its destroyed garage door. "He's probably still in there. With a gun."

"Shouldn't we run?" Genevieve asked.

"You think you can?" Cassia's brain felt weird and fuzzy. She wanted to throw up. She thought she'd fall to the ground if she tried to run now. Whether it was from the exhaust fumes or the crash, it really didn't matter. What mattered was staying safe.

Genevieve slowly shook her head. She looked ill.

Cassia pulled her cell phone from the snow pants, unlocked

it, and handed it to Genevieve. "Call the cops." Then she put the truck in neutral and turned the ignition. The engine whined once and then nothing. She tried again, giving it gas. It roared to life. She put it in gear and pushed the gas pedal. It moved forward jerkily, breaking through bits of two by four and brick wall then stopped, caught on something.

"Turn on the lights," Genevieve said, pointing ahead. A figure in the road walked toward them.

"Oh man," Cassia said. She felt around the dashboard of the truck and flicked all the levers she could find. Finally, she found the headlights. They flooded the parking lot and street ahead with the blue white light.

The man in the red and black check jacket walked toward them.

"Does he have the gun?" Cassia asked, panicking. Of course he had the gun.

"Go, go, go!" Genevieve yelled. She pointed at the steering wheel.

Cassia put the truck in reverse and backed up further into the shop, broken glass falling from the window as the truck forced its way further in. She put it in first but kept the clutch in.

"Hold on," Cassia said. Genevieve nodded and braced.

Now the man was on the grass between the road and the strip mall parking lot. Cassia stared at him as she gripped the steering wheel tightly and floored the gas. She let the clutch out and the truck popped forward and broke free of the salon. It raced across the parking lot. Cassia pulled off the gas and veered away from the guy with a squeal of the tires. If she turned too quickly, the truck would tip over.

The man saw the truck coming toward him and scrambled in a panic back to the rental building. He only made it a few feet before the massive vehicle flew by him, sending his hat flying. He stumbled to the ground.

Cassia swung the truck around to the right and drove toward town. She didn't stop at the mega-grocery store.

"Did you get help?" Cassia asked, glancing at the phone in Genevieve's hand

"Oh no, I panicked," Genevieve said. She held the phone up to her ear. "They hung up. I called 911."

"Try again," Cassia said.

"It's locked." Genevieve held the phone out to Cassia.

"Do the emergency call thing," Cassia said as she looked in the rearview mirror. She couldn't see if the guy was coming or not. She drove another block, managing to avoid a car that cut in front of her to pull into the Buddy's Fried Chicken's driveway.

Half a block ahead a four-way stoplight showed red in their direction. They were not far enough away from that maniac. Cassia did not want to slow down, much less stop. A white pickup truck crossed the road at the intersection, but there was no other traffic coming except for one car a block down. Cassia did a double take on the car.

"We are so lucky," she said. She gunned the gas in the truck, sending it through the red light and into the intersection in front of the car that was now almost at the lights.

"Cassia!" Genevieve yelled. She grabbed the roof handle on the truck and braced herself even though they were not going to hit anything.

The car, a county sheriff, flicked on his flashers and sirens and came roaring after Cassia and Genevieve in the truck.

With a sigh of relief, Cassia pulled over to let the sheriff come up behind them. His blue and reds in her rearview mirror were the best things she'd ever seen.

———

Cassia sat perched on the backseat of a sheriff's cruiser outside the ruined hair salon, the door open and a blanket around her shoulders. She held a steaming cup of coffee, sipping it occasionally, and watching everyone around her.

Five sheriff vehicles plus an ambulance, all with lights blazing, filled the parking lot. Two more sat in the rental company's driveway, well back from the destruction of the torn door. Half a dozen pickup trucks lined the street while good old boys got out to help with the cleanup.

The deputies walked in and out of the salon, taking notes. Someone was on a radio reporting the situation while dispatch worked to track down the building's owner.

Genevieve, her own blanket around her shoulders, talked animatedly with an old lady who had walked over from the mega-grocery store to see what was going on. She'd recovered with the first cup of coffee and the once-over from the cute ambulance driver and was now anxious to tell anyone who'd listen the story, blow by blow.

Deputy Chester paced anxiously between Genevieve and Cassia, checking that they were all right. He didn't dare ask or offer any more coffee after Sheriff Andrews had testily told him to knock it off.

"You're in a lot of trouble, young lady," Sheriff Andrews said. He looked down at Cassia perched on the edge of the backseat. His jaw clenched, the jaw muscles highlighted in the parking lot lights.

"It wasn't our fault," Cassia said. The first time she told him that, her voice had cracked with a bit of a whine. Now she was too exhausted to even give it that.

"How could this not be your fault? *You* stole the truck. *You* drove it into this building, and *you* used it to run a red light in front of Deputy Chester."

"I did," Cassia said in a small voice.

Sheriff Andrews threw his hands up and looked around as if someone was going to come explain it to him.

"He had a gun. He was going to kill us."

"But he didn't shoot you."

"No. He tried to suffocate us, with exhaust—" Cassia said.

"But you said it wasn't your fault because he had a gun," Sheriff Andrews said, growing frustrated.

"Well, at first it was the gun, and then later it was the gun again, but in between, he tried to suffocate us with gas. That's why we drove through the door," Cassia said, trailing off as she heard herself.

"Right. He locked you inside the building, turned on the truck, then locked the cab door and left you to die in the garage."

Cassia nodded.

"Well, how did you get in the truck?"

Cassia pointed to Genevieve, who was still talking to the old lady. "She opened it with a piece of string."

"A piece of string? Are you kidding me?!" Sheriff Andrews said, his voice so loud everyone around them looked. "Do I look like an idiot?" he asked Cassia, his face turning an interesting shade of red.

"No," she said. "No idiots here. I don't know how she did it. Ask her." She pointed at Genevieve.

Genevieve, seemingly oblivious to Sheriff Andrews' temper, came over and smiled. "I did. Mandy got sick of me calling and interrupting her shows, so she took pity on me, and herself, and showed me how to open my own car with tooth floss when I lock myself out. Nowadays I keep the card of it in all my pockets. Saves me a ton of money."

Sheriff Andrews' mouth opened and shut as he looked at Genevieve and at Cassia. "Show me," he finally said in a croaking voice.

"Do you have any floss?" Genevieve asked.

"No!" Sheriff Andrews yelled.

"I used all mine up over there," Genevieve said, pointing to the rental building. "When I get another piece, I can show you any time. I mean, they have guys with videos on the internets doing demonstrations of how to do it and stuff. You should know. Don't people steal cars using tooth floss?"

Sheriff Andrews scowled at her. Cassia looked down to keep from giggling.

"Did you catch the guy?" Genevieve asked, pointing to the rental building. "He really did try to kill us."

"All we have on that is your word, and this one is already under suspicion of murder," Sheriff Andrews said, motioning to Cassia.

"I told you, I recorded everything on my phone, but I dropped it in the garage," Genevieve said.

Sheriff Andrews crossed his arms and looked skeptical.

A deputy crossed the parking lot and walked up to Sheriff Andrews, pieces of a damaged phone in his hand. "Sheriff, we found the cell phone she said was over there."

Sheriff Andrews looked at the phone, then at Cassia and Genevieve. "Don't go anywhere." He walked off, motioning for the deputy to follow him.

Cassia flopped back on the seat. Half an hour later, Sheriff Andrews sent Cassia and Genevieve home in the back of separate squad cars. They were to get all-night guards until the guy was found. Genevieve had convinced him to let her open her phone and play the recording. Luckily, the phone still worked.

Cassia unlocked the front door to the mansion and waved good night to the deputy outside. He had refused her offer of coffee, holding up a huge thermos, and waved her off to bed.

Miss Mansfield wove around her ankles, meowing plaintively.

"It's great to see you too," Cassia said and bent down to pet the black cat. Miss Mansfield blinked at her and then trotted back off to the kitchen. Cassia followed.

All three of Miss Mansfield's dishes were empty.

"Holy cow, Miss Mansfield. You were hungry today." Cassia gathered the dishes and put them in the sink to soak. She filled several more and refreshed Miss Mansfield's water. She opened the freezer but nothing looked appealing. She was too tired to eat. Shutting the freezer again, Cassia trudged off to her bedroom and flopped in her bed and promptly fell asleep.

———

Cassia woke to banging on the front door, a familiar sound now. She groaned, then looked around for her phone and finally found it stuck deep in the pocket of the snow pants she was still wearing. Her mouth tasted terrible, and she was completely soaked in sweat from sleeping in all her clothes.

The phone screen was blank. The battery was completely dead.

The banging at the front door got louder.

"Fine, fine. I'm coming," Cassia said, pushing herself off the bed. She plugged in her phone and ran her hands through her hair as she shuffled off to the front door. Light streamed in the windows of the hallway.

She checked the peephole. Outside, Deputy Chester stood on the front stoop.

Cassia opened the door. "Good morning," she said. At his confused look, she asked, "What time is it?"

"One p.m., Miss Lemon."

It was already afternoon. No wonder Cassia felt sore and uncomfortable. She probably hadn't moved from her position all morning.

They stood there awkwardly for a moment.

"What's up?" Cassia asked.

"Oh, Sheriff Andrews wants you to come to the station. No one could get a hold of you this morning."

It must be important if Sheriff Andrews had sent Deputy Chester out to get her.

Cassia scratched her back and looked around. "Do I have time to change? Maybe get a quick shower?"

"Well—" Deputy Chester said, uncertain.

"Please?" Cassia pleaded. There was no way she could go downtown without at least a quick rinse.

"Okay," Deputy Chester said, relenting.

Cassia got him set up in the kitchen with a cup of coffee and some muffins from the freezer, fed Miss Mansfield, then went off to shower and find out what fate awaited her downtown.

CHAPTER 27

Cassia got ready in record time. The sun felt great on her wet hair as she and Deputy Chester left the mansion. He even let her play with the lights on his squad car while they were still on mansion property. It all seemed like a good sign.

The gloomy overcast clouds from yesterday had cleared completely. Birds sang, and squirrels ran across the mansion grounds. Cassia stared out the window as Deputy Chester drove them into town.

When they got to the station, Cassia was surprised to see Nate Perauski, her lawyer, leaning on the wall outside, waiting. He had on a black tracksuit and looked much different than he did in his normal work clothes. He gave her a big smile.

"Heard you had some excitement last night," he said.

"I did," Cassia said, getting out of the squad car. "Why are you here?"

"I couldn't get a hold of you this morning, and in light of everything we talked about, I thought it quickest to call the sheriff. He filled me in and told me you'd be coming down here soon."

Of course he did. Cassia wrinkled her nose.

"Sorry, phone died," Cassia said. "What's up? Did you find out anything at the county records?"

"Did I ever," Nate said as he pushed off the wall. "Remember what I told you about rights?"

Cassia nodded.

"Well, Mildred Mandress did sell the timber rights for one season about two years ago. The contract was open for renewal, but no renewal was ever filed."

"So what they were doing was legal?" Cassia asked.

"For one year, yes, but this year, no. The rights transferred ended eight months ago because there was no renewal on record with the county. They might've been betting on no one checking on the time limit of the license. If it was good for one year, people might assume it was good for the next year too," Nate said. "Whoever was doing the harvesting would also probably try to plead confusion with the contract if busted. That seems to be a common tactic, even though ignorance is no excuse in the eyes of the law."

So it had been illegal.

"That's good news," Cassia said, relieved to be backed up by the documents.

Nate chuckled. "Just you wait. The good news has just started." He opened the door to the station and motioned for Cassia to enter.

———

Cassia sat in the uncomfortable wooden chair in front of Sheriff Andrews' desk. It was spotless, as somehow she knew it would be. His nameplate was perfectly centered, and even the stapler was precisely placed to one side at a sharp ninety degree angle to the name plate. Cassia wondered if he measured where everything was with a ruler to make sure they were properly placed.

Deputy Chester stood to one side, along with a thin man Cassia had never seen before, wearing a black suit and an old-fashioned hat.

Nate sat next to Cassia. He had said it was good news. It had better be.

Sheriff Andrews cleared his throat and looked uncomfortable. "Miss Lemon, it has been an interesting night." He glanced up at the man with the hat, actually looking uncertain for once. "It seems you might be eligible for a reward."

A reward?

"What? I mean, how?" Cassia asked. Not that she didn't want a reward, but she was confused.

"It's… uh, complicated," Sheriff Andrews said.

The man with the hat stepped forward. "If I might, Sheriff?"

Sheriff Andrews nodded.

The man with the hat turned to Cassia. "My name is Thomas Rivers. I'm with the federal bureau that investigates art crimes. Thanks to the hard work of Sheriff Andrews here, we have now apprehended one of our most infamous art thieves. As we speak now they're being transported to the Twin Cities to be held for extradition."

Art thief? This was not helping at all. Cassia searched the faces of Deputy Chester, Sheriff Andrews and Thomas Rivers.

"How does this have anything to do with me?" she asked.

"I believe her most recent disguise was posing as a housekeeper at the Mandress mansion," Thomas said.

"Sarah? She's a notorious art thief?" Cassia's voice cracked.

"And a lover of disguise. She has no need for more money and just does this for fun," Thomas said.

"What does that have to do with the mansion?"

Thomas stared at Cassia, giving her a minute to think about it.

Cassia thought for a long minute about the mansion, and how empty most of it felt. The first floor looked right for an empty new house. What had it looked like before it had been remodeled, and who was responsible for that?

"Sarah took artwork out of the house," Cassia answered.

Thomas nodded. "Correct."

"Is that why it looked so empty?" Cassia asked. "The whole first floor was remodeled into a modern style, but the second and third floors were not…"

Thomas leaned against Sheriff Andrews' desk, not seeing the glare from the sheriff behind him. "We think she got rushed on this job. The normal scheme is to get in somehow in a trusted role and go from there. She's a nurse, so we were looking for private nurses, not housekeepers."

Cassia remembered the hospital bed and equipment on the second floor. "She nursed Mrs. Mandress?"

The man shook his head. "Not Mildred Mandress, no. Apparently, she came in to help Rose Johnson, the old housekeeper. I'm sure she made herself indispensable to Mrs. Mandress and finagled her new position when Rose Johnson died."

"So all that remodeling and missing things—"

"Was an excuse to take things out of the house under the guise of a remodel. I'm sure she told Mrs. Mandress she was protecting the items and just helping." Thomas said. "Mrs. Mandress dying in the middle of the job was probably unexpected. I'm not sure if the probationary period in the will came from Mrs. Mandress, or from Sarah, but it was one way for Sarah to stay on working in the house for a bit longer. It is probably the best Sarah could do in the short time she had from when Mrs. Mandress became ill to the time she died."

Cassia looked down at her hands, trying to imagine everything that happened the last few years of Mrs. Mandress's life.

"But Sarah had been working there for two years. That seems like a long time for a con," Cassia said.

Thomas shrugged his shoulders. "People entertain themselves in all sorts of ways."

Cassia glanced at Sheriff Andrews glowering in his seat behind Thomas. "Okay, I guess that makes sense, but I'm still not getting what that has to do with me and that crazy guy who tried to kill us. And Brody Johnson.

"That crazy guy," Sheriff Andrews said, "was Ken Smith—"

"Real name Mark Billet," Thomas said, interrupting. He didn't see Sheriff Andrews' annoyance at his interruption, but Cassia did. She had to look down again to stifle a giggle. "Billet wanted more of a cut than Sarah was giving him. Apparently logging was something Sarah had wrangled out of Mrs. Mandress to try to silence Billet."

"And Brody Johnson?" Cassia asked.

"An accident. Well, an accident that never would have happened if he hadn't encountered Mark Billet in the tower while Brody was trying to find something to sell to make money," Thomas explained. "Brody ran out of a window and across the roof to escape the tower and slipped, choking on his own scarf. Billet said it was storming that night and difficult to see. He didn't know until later that the kid died."

Genevieve had said it stormed that night. Cassia had slept right through it.

"So he knew it was an accident but didn't say anything?" Cassia asked.

"Yes. Beside implicating himself if he came forward, it would remove the suspicion from you. If you were gone and the house went to the state, no one would know of the lost artwork, or the illegal logging. The state doesn't have the resources to track all that," Thomas said.

Sheriff Andrews nodded, grudgingly agreeing.

"How do you know all this?" Cassia asked, scanning the faces around her.

Sheriff Andrews cleared his throat. "My men apprehended Ken Smith—"

"Mark Billet," Thomas said.

"Mark Billet," Sheriff Andrews continued, "early this morning. After showing him the video evidence we had, he was more than happy to point the finger at Sarah in exchange for some leniency. Cooperation credit."

"That all happened while I was sleeping?" Cassia asked.

"The arrests and confessions, yes, but we've been looking for Sarah for a long time," Thomas said

Nate, sitting next to her, patted her hand. "You did quite a bit last night, too. You and Genevieve."

"Genevieve gets a reward also?" Cassia asked.

"Of course." Thomas smiled. "We've already talked to her by phone this morning."

"Hopefully the reward will cover the repair bills," Sheriff Andrews muttered to himself, but still loud enough for Cassia to hear. Alarmed, she turned and looked at Nate. He shook his head.

"Come see me later," Nate said.

Cassia slumped back in her chair, dazed by all the information. A heaviness she hadn't known she was carrying lifted off her chest when she realized she was no longer a suspect in a murder investigation.

CHAPTER 28

Cassia sat at the island in the mansion kitchen, sipping a mug of tea and looking around the beautiful space that she couldn't believe was really going to be hers. The remains of a frozen meal sat on the plate in front of her, a strange reminder of Sarah, who had been both kind and rude, all while stealing from Cassia and her family. Miss Mansfield curled on the stool next to Cassia, purring loudly.

Nate had taken her home, promising to help find the keys to the cars in the Mandress garage so she wouldn't have to bike everywhere. She'd have to get her bike back too. That was still in the back of Genevieve's car. Nate had also said the probationary period in the will would probably stand, no matter what, but now Cassia didn't have someone actively working against her.

Getting up from the stool, Cassia took her tea and walked through the mansion, looking at all the empty spaces not filled by the sparse furniture. She wondered what had been there before. Thomas had told her they had a lead on a warehouse where a lot of the stuff from the mansion had been taken. Some of it might have been sold already, but there was a good chance she would get most of the items back. Cassia was excited but also overwhelmed at the thought of dealing with more things. She might have to get a real housekeeper to help.

Cassia climbed the stairs to the second floor and then went down the hall to the stairs to the massive third floor bedroom. The beautiful room that must have been her aunt's.

She hadn't locked the doors since she'd gone exploring with Genevieve. Pulling open the beautiful enormous door, she stared into the room of the woman who she was related to but had never known. Why had her parents hidden this from her? Did they even know of Mildred Mandress and the estate here?

Cassia walked into the room and stared around. Most of this furniture was old and expensive looking. These must have been some of the things Sarah hadn't had a chance to get out of the house yet. Cassia stared at the walls, this time knowing what she was looking for and rewarded with spotting the faint outlines of where pictures had once been. Sarah had started looting this room, but hadn't completed the job.

Cassia sat down in the chair where Genevieve had found the envelope in the note. Had Mildred known what was going on in her own home? Did she know to hide the note for Cassia to find? Cassia knew she was lucky Genevieve had found it before Sarah whisked away this furniture too.

Miss Mansfield walked around the room, having followed Cassia, rubbing on chair legs and purring contentedly. She jumped on to Cassia's lap and curled into a crescent, kneading at Cassia's belly.

Everything had been wrapped up so neatly, except for the note stashed under the chair in this room. It bothered Cassia to not understand what it meant. She was sure the series of numbers was the speed of light, but what did that mean to Aunt Mildred? What was it supposed to mean to Cassia? She looked at it every day in her studies and running her formulas over and over again from—.

Cassia sat up quickly, disturbing Miss Mansfield who complained with a loud meow. Cassia set down the tea mug on a nearby shelf and ran out the door and down the stairs. She ran through the hallway on the second floor and then down the front stairway, down the hall and finally into the beautiful library she'd not had a chance to explore because of all the excitement.

How were the books ordered? Cassia scanned a nearby shelf. She'd lucked out. They were ordered by title. She scanned down past the As, the Bs, until she reached the Ss. She found the book she was looking for, *The Speed of Light*. She pulled the book from the shelf, her hand shaking.

Grabbing the thick tome, she opened the book and fanned through the pages and then held it upside down. An envelope fell out. Genevieve would have been proud. It wasn't a book full of cash, but it might be something much more valuable to Cassia.

Putting down the book, Cassia grabbed the envelope and turned it over. In a beautiful longhand script it said "Cassia Lemon". Cassia put her hand to her mouth, her eyes watering. Going to a nearby chair at one of the library tables, she sat down and stared at the envelope. Finally, she got the courage to slip a finger under the edge of the envelope and open it, being careful not to tear it.

Inside sat a single thin sheet of parchment paper, folded over once.

Cassia pulled out the paper and opened it. In the same beautiful script written on the outside of the envelope was a handwritten note.

Dear Cassia,

    Oh my dear, how many times I have dreamed of you. I hope you are well. I've always wondered how you were and wished to speak to you, but for reasons that make little sense now, I could not. With your success in finding this note, I wish that you may also be successful in unraveling what is going on with this mansion. I miss my dear friend Rose and hold on to the hope that you can rectify what I was not able to. I cannot risk putting too much information here, but I've seeded missives all over the universe that is this mansion.

Know that you were much loved, even if I could not tell you in person.

Love, Aunt Mildred

So Mildred did know, both about the mansion and about Cassia. Now more than ever, Cassia wished that she could turn back time, not just for her parents but also to get to know the woman who had been her aunt.

Cassia sat in the library for several hours as the sun dipped over the horizon and set. Finally, she rose from her chair and carefully reset the book on the shelf with the note tucked safely back inside it. Monday she was going to call the law firm in New York and she wasn't going to give up until she found out why Aunt Mildred had left her that number.

ALSO BY SHAW COLLINS

CASSIA LEMON MYSTERIES

Cat on a Wire

Cat Dancer

Cat and Mouse

———

www.ShawCollins.com

ABOUT THE AUTHOR

Shaw Collins is owned by another perfect Miss Mansfield and lives in the frozen tundra of the upper Midwest whilst dreaming of warm summer nights.

9 781951 098162